"I have some roses for you," Charley said, holding the bouquet out to Edith.

Unfortunately, she had a potted plant in her hands, so there was no way she could accept them.

Charley pulled his arm back. "I'll just hold them for you."

"Thank you. They're lovely," she said.

"Not as lovely as you."

"That's so kind."

Charley took a deep breath and made his dive. "It's not kind. I want to marry you," he said, all in a rush so he could breathe again.

"Marry me? *Marry me?*"

"I know it's unexpected," Charley said, "but I just had to—"

"It's very gallant of you, but there's no need. I don't feel bad at all anymore."

"You think I'm proposing to make you feel better?"

"That's why you're so special," Edith said before she turned and walked up the street.

Charley had no idea what to do now.

Books by Janet Tronstad

Love Inspired

*An Angel for Dry Creek
*A Gentleman for Dry Creek
*A Bride for Dry Creek
*A Rich Man for Dry Creek
*A Hero for Dry Creek
*A Baby for Dry Creek
*A Dry Creek Christmas
*Sugar Plums for Dry Creek
*At Home in Dry Creek
**The Sisterhood of the Dropped Stitches
*Shepherds Abiding in Dry Creek
**A Dropped Stitches Christmas
*Dry Creek Sweethearts
**A Heart for the Dropped Stitches
*A Dry Creek Courtship

*Dry Creek
**The Sisterhood of the Dropped Stitches

JANET TRONSTAD

grew up on a small farm in central Montana. One of
her favorite things to do was to visit her grandfather's
bookshelves, where he had a large collection of Zane
Grey novels. She's always loved a good story.
Today Janet lives in Pasadena, California, where she
is a full-time writer.

A Dry Creek Courtship
Janet Tronstad

Steeple
Hill®

Published by Steeple Hill Books™

STEEPLE HILL BOOKS

Steeple
Hill®

ISBN-13: 978-0-373-87495-8
ISBN-10:   0-373-87495-2

A DRY CREEK COURTSHIP

He who finds a wife finds a good thing
and obtains favor from the Lord.
—*Proverbs* 18:22

This book is dedicated with a thankful heart
to my wonderful editor, Joan Marlow Golan.
She is the best.

Chapter One

The disturbing letter was safely hidden in the pocket of Edith Hargrove's apron. It had arrived along with the rest of her mail in Dry Creek, Montana, early last week, but it had not seemed right to stack a letter like that with the regular mail on the sideboard in her dining room. It wasn't a bill or a reminder for an appointment or even a notice from Social Security. So she kept it close to her, as though this might in some way tell her more about the woman who'd had the astonishing nerve to send it.

Edith had read the letter so many times she could almost feel the texture of the paper against her fingers even when she wasn't holding it. She kept wondering if she'd overlooked some clue.

She was still thinking about it as she sat on a stool on her front porch waiting for her recently married daughter, Doris June, to cut her hair. The morning was overcast and a bit chilly. It was quiet in the small town of Dry Creek. Edith shifted on the stool and heard the faint crinkle of paper in her pocket.

She couldn't tell anyone about the letter, of course. The scented envelope had been hand-addressed to Mr. Harold Hargrove, her deceased husband. At first, Edith thought it was one of those letters that had been lost in the mail for a decade. She'd heard about letters like that and, since Harold had been dead for fifteen years, it seemed like that was the only possible explanation. But this letter had been postmarked in Los Angeles just a few days before she received it.

There was no return address. Edith considered giving the envelope back to the post office without opening it until she remembered the days when she could barely afford to buy a stamp. Anyone who paid to mail a letter deserved to have it read by someone, even if it was just the intended man's widow. After all these years, Edith doubted there was anything in a letter that could disquiet her anyway.

She hadn't counted on unfolding that piece of scented white stationery and seeing the woman's signature at the bottom—Jasmine Hunter. Edith had felt her breath stop for a moment when she first saw the name. It was causing her to stiffen up even now just remembering it.

"You're sure you're okay with this?" Doris June asked as she wrapped an old dish towel around her mother's shoulders. The towel would keep the trimmed hairs off both of them. "You can change your mind, you know. You've never wanted me to cut your hair in the fall before. You always say you're too busy to do it and that you'll wait until the snow flies."

Dead leaves were scattered all over Edith's front lawn, but snow was weeks, maybe months, away.

Edith forced herself to relax. "I can't run around looking like a scarecrow just because the weather hasn't turned."

Doris June gave her mother a startled look. "Your hair never looks that bad."

Edith glanced up and gave her daughter a reassuring smile. The letter had definitely put her on edge. She thought she could still smell that envelope even though it was tucked away in her apron.

She hadn't recognized the scent at first. But of course it was jasmine, the strong, mysterious scent that seemed to go with a sophisticated woman in a way that Edith's simple rose water never could. She'd avoided the perfume even before she'd heard about Jasmine Hunter, the woman Harold had—what could she say?—slept with, succumbed to, maybe even loved some forty years ago.

After the first burst of passionate confession, Harold had refused to talk about it for weeks. He said Jasmine was moving away and that was the end of that. Of course, it hadn't been the end of anything. The woman might have gone, but the pain of knowing Harold had betrayed their marriage vows was there to stay.

Edith brought her mind back to the present. "All I'm saying is my hair could look better."

Her daughter was quietly taking the pins out of Edith's hair. The hair itself reminded her of what she'd lost. Harold had always claimed he liked her soft brown hair pulled back in the simple bun that she wore and she'd believed him…until the affair. He'd given her the same compliments after it all happened, but she'd stopped hearing them. She'd been too proud to go chasing after a new hairstyle, but she knew something somewhere had been wrong or he wouldn't have turned to another woman.

Edith had never met Jasmine, but she'd always pictured her as having a fancy hairdo and some kind of exotic, sultry eyeliner. Maybe she'd even had a black hat with a sweeping wide brim. Hats were fashionable back then and elegant women were pictured wearing them in glossy magazines that Edith couldn't afford to buy on her farm-wife budget.

Edith had never looked good in a hat; the only ones she'd ever owned were the ones she wore for pulling weeds in her garden. She doubted Jasmine had pulled a weed in her life. She probably wore her hats to tea parties or presidential inaugurations or the Emmys on television. Following Harold's confession, Edith had pictured the other woman as being everything she herself wasn't and those pictures had grown with time until the real Jasmine Hunter couldn't possibly have been as exciting as she was in Edith's mind.

At the time, Edith had searched for the perfect word to name the affair between Harold and the woman. She knew it wouldn't change anything, though she thought it might help. But she'd never found a single word big enough to contain the pain. This thing had broken her heart.

It had taken her a decade to rebuild herself enough to truly forgive Harold. The nameless pain from the affair itself and her resulting insecurity had left a dark hole in their marriage. She didn't know if they would have made it through without the help of God and their elderly pastor. Harold had grown more distant from

God in those years, but she'd grown closer. She'd had no choice really. She had to rely on Him for everything.

"Well, you're usually so busy," Doris June said as she paused in her movements. "Your hair can always wait. You don't have time to spend hours in front of the mirror anyway."

At first, Edith had thought that was part of the problem. She had always been able to think of a million things she should be doing instead of fussing with her appearance. Back at the time of the affair, she had been taking care of Doris June who had been little more than a toddler. That hadn't left much time for extras like hairstyling.

Edith had always looked pleasant, but she knew she wasn't beautiful in the way some women were. Her jaw was too square and her green eyes too direct for conventional beauty. She had a face men trusted, not one that inspired them to write poetry. Besides, it had seemed pointless to spend hours in front of a mirror when there were so many things to do for her family and others.

After Harold's affair, she had become keenly aware of the troubles in other people's lives. She knew what it was to be alone and needy. She'd started healing her own heart by helping other people.

Eventually, the questions she'd been asking herself had faded away. She finally realized that Harold hadn't gone to bed with another woman because of her hairstyle or something she had said in a thoughtless moment. His decision to be unfaithful was simply that—his decision. All she could do in her life was be the person God had made her to be. And, if He had

made her plain and serviceable, so be it. Her decision
to wholeheartedly accept herself was what gradually
allowed her marriage to mend.

Even now, Edith had too many things to do to worry
overmuch about her hair. Like today, she should be in
her kitchen boiling her Mason jars so she'd be ready
when Charley Nelson finally brought over the annual
bucket of chokecherries he always picked for her. She
boiled the jars twice and, ordinarily, those jars would
have had their first boil days ago. Charley was late with
the berries and she'd just realized it this morning. She
needed to make the jelly soon if she was going to be
ready for the harvest dinner at church.

Edith wondered if Charley knew about Harold's
affair. The Nelson family had always been their closest
neighbors when they were on the farm. Charley made
some extra money working with the local vet so he
managed to stay home on his farm that hard winter
when most of the other men around had been forced
to take temporary jobs in Billings to keep up with their
bank payments. The roads were so bad and the distance
to Billings so far that Harold had rented a motel room
for several nights each week during the two months.
It was then that he'd met Jasmine.

Edith decided Charley couldn't have known about
the affair. Harold had sworn to her he hadn't said
anything to anyone except the pastor, and he'd only
talked to the pastor at her request. Edith had been
adamant at the time that she didn't ever want Doris
June to find out about the affair. She was a sweet little
girl and she adored her daddy. Today, of course,
families would talk about something like that, but back

then they didn't. Everyone suffered in as much silence as they could manage.

"Getting a haircut is important," Edith said. She had forced herself to call Doris June this morning and ask for her help. "Women need to be well-groomed if they're going to be out and about with people."

Doris June finished taking the pins out of her mother's hair. "I'm always happy to cut your hair for you."

Hair framed Edith's face. It was coarse instead of soft after all the years and much more gray than brown. "I thought this time I'd have you do it shorter. Something over the ears."

Edith had been too stubborn to change her hairstyle for Harold, but she felt a need to update it for this other woman. Jasmine Hunter was coming to Montana and wanted to meet and talk. That, in addition to an address printed on the stationery, was all the letter had said.

"No problem, I'll just—" Doris June sputtered to a stop. "Did you say *over the ears?*"

Edith nodded. "I've worn my hair pulled back in this bun since I married your father. That was fifty years ago. Styles have changed since then."

Edith had sent her answer to the letter in the mail several days ago. She explained that Harold had died, but that she would be willing to meet Jasmine and talk if that would be "an acceptable alternative." Edith had struggled with the words and been pleased when she thought of "acceptable alternative." It sounded so businesslike and not at all like the words of a woman who'd been betrayed.

Of course, she knew she would have been within her rights to simply not answer the letter. No one could blame her if she just copied the address from inside the letter on the envelope and sent it back through the post office with a big Deceased stamped across the front. But it hadn't taken Edith long to realize this would probably be her only chance to face the woman who had haunted her marriage. Maybe those images she'd had in her mind for years would finally be laid to rest if she met Jasmine.

"I know how long you've worn that bun. That's why you should think about it before you cut your hair short," Doris June said as she started to comb her mother's hair.

"What's to think about? Your father—bless his soul— is the one who liked it this way. At least that's what he always said. And he's not around to notice anymore."

It was possible this Hunter woman wouldn't even want to talk to her, Edith thought. Jasmine might not know that Harold's wife knew about the affair. Edith may have worked up her courage for nothing.

"Well, no, but—" Doris June stopped combing and stepped around to look at her mother. "This isn't about missing Dad, is it? I know you loved him terribly. He was a wonderful man. But you're not alone now that he's gone. Lots of people will notice a new haircut. There's me. And your Sunday school class. The whole church, in fact. And I'm sure Charley will notice."

Edith managed to nod. She wondered if she'd need to tell Doris June that her father wasn't as perfect as she'd always thought. Edith would rather have her heart broken all over again than cause her daughter that kind of pain.

Doris June seemed to be waiting for some response so Edith said, "I know."

And she did know she could count on people to care about what happened with her. Charley was her best friend. The two of them had fallen into the habit of looking out for each other after his wife had died. They'd started doing it when they both lived on their farms and continued when Edith moved to her house in Dry Creek.

Still, Charley wouldn't pay too much attention. It was only a haircut. And she wanted it to stay that way. Which meant she needed to get her daughter's mind on something else before Doris June started asking why her mother had felt this sudden need to change the way she wore her hair.

"Of course, Charley has other things to worry about. He's growing a moustache," Edith said.

"Charley? Are you sure?"

Edith nodded. She didn't think Charley would mind that she was using him to distract her daughter.

"Well, I'll be—I wonder if he's planning to start dating."

"I don't think—" Edith blinked in surprise. Charley, dating! He never dated. Then she remembered that Harold had grown a moustache when he'd been courting her. It's what men of her generation did when they wanted to attract the attention of a particular woman. They were like peacocks displaying their feathers.

For the first time since she'd gotten that letter, Edith completely forgot about Jasmine Hunter. She wasn't sure she liked the thought of Charley dating someone. It was unreasonable, of course, but she had gotten used to the way things were between her and Charley. She depended on him. If he started dating someone, everything would change.

"I'm sure he would have said something," Edith said. By now, she was frowning a little. "Wouldn't he?"

Doris June shrugged. "I don't know. I haven't seen him at your place much lately. You two aren't arguing, are you?"

Now that her daughter mentioned it, Edith realized Charley hadn't been spending as much time at her place as he had in the past. She would have noticed sooner if she hadn't been so preoccupied with her own problems.

"No, Charley and I are fine." She hoped.

"That's good." Doris moved around and started combing her mother's hair again.

"You're not worried about something yourself, are you?" Edith thought her daughter was combing her hair longer than usual.

"Nothing big," Doris June said a little cautiously as she kept combing. "It's just that, if you want your hair that short, it needs to be cut by someone who knows what they're doing. I think we should go to the beauty place in Miles City."

Edith turned around. "But you always cut my hair."

"Yes, and I can do a straight cut with the best of them. But that's just getting things even. What you want is a whole lot more complicated. Your hair has to curve to go over the ear."

Edith had gone to that beauty shop with Doris June so they could both get their hair styled for the wedding. Doris June had married Charley's son, Curt, some months ago. They'd been high school sweethearts who'd been apart for over twenty-five years before Edith and Charley brought them back together. Edith thought it was the best thing she and Charley had ever done. It was also the last thing they'd done together.

She wondered who Charley was hoping to impress with his moustache.

Doris June kept combing. "It wouldn't hurt you to get that deep oil treatment they offer. It's good for your hair follicles."

"My hair follicles are doing just fine, thank you." *Maybe he had met someone in Miles City. He'd been driving there a lot for one reason or another lately.*

"Hmm, maybe," Doris June said as she parted her mother's hair and clipped half of it back. "But something isn't right. You feeling okay?"

"Of course." *There was that new woman at the beauty shop.*

"Have you been sleeping okay?" Doris June asked. "I know sometimes when people get to your age they have to keep getting up during the night to—"

"I sleep just fine." *Charley might even be having that woman trim his moustache. What better way to get to know someone?*

"Good." Doris June finished combing one side of her mother's hair. "Are you taking your vitamins? I read the other day that—"

"For pity's sake, I take my vitamins."

"Well, I'm only trying to show that I'm here to help you with your problems, whatever they might be."

"I'm sorry." Edith supposed she did owe her daughter some kind of an explanation. She could hardly mention the letter or Charley's moustache. She could talk about the feelings they both prompted, though. "It's just… It's the dead leaves outside. And making the same old kind of jelly. I've been feeling like my life just isn't very exciting."

It might be selfish, but she didn't want Charley to date someone. When Harold died, she'd vowed no other man would ever make her feel the way he had. That's why she liked her friendship with Charley the way it was. She thought they were both past all that dating business.

"But everyone loves your chokecherry jelly. The whole church raves about it at the harvest dinner. It's practically a town tradition to have it."

Edith brought herself back to the conversation. What Doris said was true. Everyone in the congregation tried to provide locally grown food for the harvest dinner and Edith had brought homemade chokecherry jelly and baking powder biscuits for decades. People said they loved her biscuits and jelly.

She'd always been a good cook—in fact, that's how she'd gotten to know Harold. She'd been a teenager when she cooked for the thrashing crew that cut the Hargrove wheat one fall. Harold was nineteen; she was seventeen. She'd been speechless with awe just looking at him. He was a laughing, sculpted work of art like she saw in her textbooks. She'd thought a miracle had happened when he proposed. After they became engaged, he used to joke that he'd fallen in love with her cooking first and then with her.

She'd never dreamed at the time that there was anything wrong with what Harold had said. She'd told herself that just because a man liked her cooking, that didn't mean he didn't love her completely. Those doubts came later.

After Harold told her about his affair, she'd spent days making chokecherry jelly from the raw juice she'd canned the fall before. The bitter tartness of the berry matched the sourness of her soul. The chokecherry was one of the few fruits that grew wild in the southeastern plains of Montana and it was able to survive in the drought in a way something sweeter and softer, like a peach, couldn't.

From that winter on, Edith had always pictured Jasmine as the exotic peach and herself as the sturdy chokecherry. She was the one who belonged; she was the one who could endure the dry days with or without Harold's love.

"If it's the jelly that's troubling you, I can help you with that," Doris June said. "Just pick the day and I'll arrange my schedule. But it'll have to be soon. The harvest dinner comes up on the tenth."

That was a little over a week away.

"Charley hasn't brought me the berries."

Summer was already moving into early fall and chokecherries didn't stay on the bushes forever. Edith could already detect the musty smell of grass turning brown. The berries would be ending soon.

If she hadn't been so worried about that letter, she would have thought to remind Charley about the berries. According to the calendar, she should be making that jelly now. She wished she had finished the jelly before she got the letter. The satisfaction of seeing all those jars of dark red jelly would have eased some of her nerves.

"Maybe Charley's just off his schedule since he moved into his place in Dry Creek," Doris June said.

"He's probably so busy unpacking he doesn't even know what month it is."

"Maybe," Edith said. After the wedding, Charley had rented the old Jergenson house and moved off the farm, leaving the place to Curt, Doris June and Curt's teenage son, Brad. He claimed the small town of Dry Creek was more restful than the farm and allowed him to be closer to his friends.

Edith leaned forward so she could see down the street to the hardware store. Yes, Charley's pickup was parked out front just like it usually was unless he was out doing a small vet job. The Jergenson place was only a quarter mile from the hardware store, but Charley preferred to have his pickup with him in case he got a call about an animal.

"You don't suppose he's sick?" Doris June asked.

Edith shook her head. "He wouldn't be out in public if he was sick."

Every fall a group of men, mostly retired farmers, started to gather each morning around the potbelly stove in the middle of the hardware store. The warmth of the burning wood and the smell of the coffee brewing on the counter made these men feel right at home. The gathering was a ritual of sorts.

In the summer, the men met over at the café, where there was air-conditioning. But their hearts were with that aging stove and as soon as the fall chill was in the air, they returned like homing pigeons to the unvarnished wood chairs clustered around the old thing.

Even before Charley moved into town, he had always joined the other men around the stove when he could. That part of his behavior wasn't puzzling. What was just becoming clear to Edith, however, was that Charley was no longer making it a point to stop by her place for breakfast before settling down with the men. And he'd never forgotten her chokecherries before.

"He's not sick but something's wrong," Edith said. Maybe he knew she wouldn't like him dating.

Of course, Charley still came by to see her. It's just that he never came at meal time and he never quite seemed himself. It was like he was holding something back from her. Edith knew she was keeping a secret from Charley, but for the first time she realized he might be keeping a secret from her, too. Charley was her oldest friend and—until now—she'd assumed he confided in her as much as she confided in him.

She had a sinking feeling Charley had been trying to tell her something important for some time now. The last time he had come to her house, he had cleared his throat a dozen times, but all he'd done was repeat what he'd already said about her not driving her car outside of Dry Creek. Charley hadn't come inside her house to deliver his opinion, either. He'd stood out on the porch even though he couldn't have been comfortable in the early morning cold. She'd thought it was odd he'd come by only to tell her the same thing he'd told her many times before. He must have planned to tell her something else and couldn't.

"So, we'll wait on the haircut?" Doris June asked as she twisted the hair back into its usual bun.

Edith nodded. She had to pull her worries back and stop leaping ahead to conclusions. She didn't even know why Charley had grown that moustache for sure. Maybe it had nothing to do with dating some woman.

"Good," Doris June said as she started putting the hairpins back in place. "That gives me time to rake up those leaves for you before I head back to the farm."

"You don't need to."

"I'm glad to help out. You know that." Doris June untied the dish towel from her mother's shoulders.

After Doris June left, Edith went out on the porch to sit. Her daughter had raked the yard and brought in the Mason jars from the garage. She'd also stored the lawn mower in the shed and checked all the windows in the small room over the garage to be sure they were tightly closed. Edith rented that room out here and there and she liked to keep it ready for use. The only fall chore remaining was the jelly.

Edith stood up. She was tired of sitting at home and brooding. There was no reason she couldn't go get those chokecherries herself. Pastor Matthew had recharged the battery in her old car last week so she was finally able to drive. She'd begun to wonder if she'd ever get her car working again. She must have asked every man in town for help, but all of them, except the pastor, had said they had misplaced their jumper cables and couldn't help her.

Now that she could, she'd just drive to the coulee over by the Elkton Ranch and pick a bucket of chokecherries. Everyone knew that was the best place to pick them, even this late in the season. Big Dry Creek ran through that coulee and the soil was good. There'd be chokeberry bushes alongside the coulee going down to the creek, and cattails by the creek itself.

Edith turned to walk back inside her house so she could get ready. Now that she'd decided to do it, she was looking forward to it. The exercise would help clear her mind. All that berry-picking might even ease the arthritis in her hands. She'd wear her gardening hat, of course, and her walking shoes with thick, high socks so her legs wouldn't get scratched by the thistles that would surely be around.

Edith nodded to herself. There was nothing like a walk over some solid Montana farmland to make her remember who she was. She was a good strong woman. It was time to be reminded of that. She didn't need to fret over the actions of any man.

Chapter Two

Charley Nelson sat with his empty coffee cup in one hand. A checkerboard was laid out on the table to the right of his chair. If he looked past the woodstove, he could see through the windows of the hardware store and out to the street. He'd been looking through those windows for the past twenty minutes, waiting for Elmer Maynard to finish talking about the paint job he planned for his old white Cadillac.

Before Elmer had started talking, Charley had set up the board so they could play. Then he'd gotten a fresh, hot cup of coffee. Elmer didn't even seem to notice the board, he was so busy debating the virtues of midnight blue and ocean blue when applied to a car. Charley was amazed a man could have so many opinions about the different shades of blue yet never have any strategy when it came to a simple game of checkers.

Between the stillness out the window and the drone of Elmer's voice, Charley was almost dozing when he heard a sound in the distance. At first, he couldn't really make out the sound, but as it got louder he placed it quickly. It woke him right up. "What's that woman doing?"

Charley set his coffee cup down on the table and looked around him with a scowl. The hardware store was having a sale on nails so there were a dozen men leaning against the counter, wanting to make purchases. "I thought we all agreed no one was going to jump start that battery for Mrs. Hargrove."

Not a man dared lift his gaze to Charley and that included the salesman who was just there to bring in a new display case of shovels. He didn't even know Mrs. Hargrove.

Finally, Elmer jutted out his chin and said. "We didn't *agree*. You told us what you wanted, but that didn't mean we agreed with you."

"Yeah," a couple of the men said.

"Well, you should have enough sense to agree. All of you." Charley stared down each of the men who dared to meet his gaze. He knew Edith could make most of them do anything she wanted if she put on her Sunday-school-teacher voice. But he thought he'd impressed upon them the need to stop her from driving that beat-up old car. The thing barely ran. It was a break-down waiting to happen.

There was another moment's silence, broken only by the crackling of the wood in the stove.

"I'm the one who jump-started the battery for her," Pastor Matthew finally said from where he stood behind the counter. He'd been going over the catalogue to fill out the order form for new nails. "It seemed the Christian thing to do when she asked."

Charley's face got red but he figured he couldn't very well tell the pastor to stop acting like a Christian. Everyone knew it was his job to do things like that. Trust Edith to pick the one man in town who Charley couldn't easily scold.

"Well, I don't think it's a good idea. Not a good idea at all," Charley muttered.

"She's not a bad driver," Elmer said. "For a woman, that is."

"She's an excellent driver," Charley snapped back. "That's never been the problem. It's that car. It should have been chopped up into scrap metal years ago. The muffler is almost worn out and those windshield wipers are about to fall off."

"Well, then you should fix it up for her, if you're so worried," Elmer said.

"It would take more money to fix that car than to buy you a new Cadillac," Charley said, even though he knew it wasn't strictly true. Still, it was foolish to fix up that eyesore when it would cost less to buy a reasonable used car that a dignified woman like Edith would be proud to drive.

"She's awfully fond of that car," the pastor said from the counter. "It seems it was the last car Harold bought before he died. Memories, you know."

Charley grunted. He didn't like to speak ill of the dead, but he couldn't help it. "That man never could pick a car that was worth anything. I can't understand why she'd want to keep a rattletrap around to remind her of Harold's poor judgment when it came to cars. He always planted his wheat too early, too, but that's neither here nor there."

"Well, if you're so set on her having a new car," Elmer said as he hooked his thumbs on his suspenders, "why don't you just sic that nephew of yours on her? It's Conrad, isn't it? You told me he's adding a used car lot to that garage of his and I drove by the other day when I was in Miles City. Let him sell her something."

"She might not be able to afford a new car," the pastor cautioned.

"The ad in front of Conrad's shop said they never turn anyone away," Elmer said. "So money should be no-o-o problem."

"He got that sign from another car lot that had gone out of business," Charley said. "Conrad doesn't want to put much money into signs before he knows if he'll get any customers."

"Well, he shouldn't put up a sign if he doesn't mean it," Elmer said. "That's the worst thing he can do for business. Besides, selling something to Mrs. Hargrove would *be* business so I'd think he'd hop right on it. Everyone in the county will notice if she's driving a new car. A good word from her could bring him more customers than he'll know what to do with."

Charley reached over to get his empty coffee cup and then stood up. "I guess it couldn't hurt to talk to him." He walked over to the counter and set the cup down. "Conrad has to prove himself a salesman someday. If he can sell a car to Edith, he can sell a car to anyone."

The pastor looked up from his order form and nodded at Charley. "That woman knows her mind, all right. She won't be easy to convince if she doesn't want to be."

"Some women get a new car just because they like the color," Elmer said. "Remind your nephew to talk about color with her. The blues are always popular. Tell him to say it'll match her eyes."

"Edith's eyes are green," Charley said as he started walking to the door.

"Hey," Elmer called out, "we haven't had our game yet. Where are you going?"

"I'll be back," Charley said. "I just need to check up on that car."

Charley stood on the porch of the hardware store and looked down the road. He could see Edith's mustard-colored car in the distance, billowing out enough smoke to show that it was still moving. He shook his head as he walked over to his pickup. It wasn't easy to talk sense to a stubborn woman, but he had to try.

Edith stopped her car at the point in the road near where the coulee started to dip. Autumn came fast and furious to this part of Montana. When she got out of the car, she looked in all directions and could see the brown patches of grass that had already turned for the year. Farther out, she could see the Big Sheep Mountains.

Edith made sure her socks were pulled up as high as they could go before she took her bucket and started to the edge of the coulee. The ground sloped down gradually and she had to be careful not to slide.

She wasn't more than eight feet down the slope when she heard the sound of a vehicle stopping on the road above. She supposed it was one of the hands at the Elkton Ranch making sure she was all right. Everyone in the whole county knew her car so they wouldn't be wondering who was walking down in the coulee; they'd just be stopping to make sure she was okay.

"I'm fine," Edith called out. She was far enough down in the coulee that she couldn't see who it was that had parked. "Just going to pick some chokecherries."

"Well, that's a fool thing to be doing."

Edith didn't need to see the man to know that it was Charley up there. She hadn't seen him for two days, she thought in annoyance, and he decided now was the time to talk to her. Her daughter hadn't put the pins back in Edith's bun securely and she could feel her hair starting to pull loose. Even with the hat on her head, a person could still see her sagging hair. She probably looked frightful. Plus, the hat was yellow and she always had thought it made her face look a little green.

"You don't need to come down," Edith called back. The best thing would be if Charley just went away. Then she wouldn't need to worry about how she looked. "I'm doing fine."

She didn't know why she was suddenly worried about how she looked when it was only Charley. He knew she was a plain-featured woman with work lines on her face. He'd probably seen every one of her gardening hats over the years.

Charley stood at the top of the coulee and saw Edith slowly walking down. He could kick himself. He'd completely forgotten about picking the chokecherries. His mind had been on that old car of hers. He should have remembered she'd need those berries to make her harvest-dinner jelly.

"I'll be right there," Charley said as he started down the coulee. Edith was holding herself stiff and he wondered if her arthritis was acting up. "You don't need to be climbing down no coulees."

"I can certainly pick a few chokecherries," Edith said. "Just because I haven't done it for a few years doesn't mean I can't."

Charley noticed the woman didn't even turn around to face him. That didn't bode well.

"I'm sorry I forgot." Charley kept right on going down the side of the coulee, sidestepping instead of walking straight to keep his balance. "I can get the berries now though. Just give me a few minutes."

Charley caught up with Edith as she reached the chokecherry bushes. They were gnarled and rooted deep in the sandy soil with nothing but thistles to keep them company. Those bushes had been there for decades and each year they were red with chokecherries until the birds from Canada started picking the berries off as they flew south.

There were no red berries in sight.

"They're all gone," Charley said. The birds had already been here. The bushes were picked clean. "I'm sorry. Maybe there's some left over on that hill by the Morgan farm."

Those berries were never as plump and Charley knew that, but he saw no reason to remind Edith of that fact.

"It's all right," Edith said. "I can get by without chokecherry jelly."

Charley noticed that she still hadn't looked at him. "But you always make chokecherry jelly."

"Only because there's no peaches around."

"I'll get you some chokecherries. Don't worry," he vowed.

Edith finally turned to him. The brim of her floppy garden hat kept her face in shadow, but Charley could see the stiff curve of her lips as she gave him what would pass for a smile if he didn't know her like he did.

Charley felt miserable.

"What happened to your moustache?" Edith asked. "I thought you were growing a moustache."

Charley nodded. "I couldn't decide if it made me look better or not so I shaved it off."

"You don't need a moustache to make you look handsome," Edith said firmly. She sounded relieved. "You've got a fine face."

"Really?" Charley smiled. "I thought maybe I could use a change."

"Well, sometimes change isn't what we need at all."

Charley knew Edith didn't like change. But the same old things weren't always good, either. "If you ask me, we absolutely need to change sometimes. Like with…" Charley lost his nerve. He couldn't say anything about the changes he'd like to make between the two of them. "Cars. There comes a time when a person needs a new car."

Edith nodded. "If you want a new car, you should get one."

"I didn't mean *me.* I meant you. Besides, what's wrong with my pickup? It can still pull a horse trailer if I need to move an animal. And I've just got the driver seat broken in the way I like it."

"Then you know how attached a person gets to their car. I don't know if I'd be able to drive a different car."

Charley shifted his feet. "The new cars steer easier than that old Ford you have. You'd like a new one if you'd give it a chance and take it out for a test drive."

"My old car does fine for me."

Charley snorted. "Just because Harold bought you that car—"

"He didn't buy it for me," Edith interrupted. "It was his car. He bought it for himself."

"Well, all I'm saying is that Harold wouldn't expect you to keep it forever. Not when you consider everything."

Edith drew in her breath. "What do you mean by that?"

Maybe Charley knew more about the past than she thought. Did he know about Jasmine?

Charley looked at her. "Just what I said. When you consider the muffler and the battery and the windshield wipers that don't work. Harold would not expect you to keep the thing."

"Oh." Edith put her hand up to steady her hat against a breeze. The movement made her feet slip a little along the side of the coulee.

"But that's why you keep that old car, isn't it? Because it reminds you of Harold?" Charley didn't know why it annoyed him that Edith was so loyal to her dead husband. She even had that locket the man had given her tied to the rearview mirror in the car. Charley knew it had both of their pictures in it because that's what lockets were for. He had grieved for his wife deeply when she died, but he hadn't set up any memorial for her in his pickup.

"There's nothing wrong with my car," Edith said. "I keep it because it gets me where I'm going."

"Barely."

Edith lifted her head. "The world would be a better place if people didn't throw away things that still worked. Just look at how many landfills there are in this country. People need to fix things instead of throw them away."

"I don't think they put old cars in landfills." Especially not around here, Charley thought. He didn't even think there was a landfill within a hundred miles of where they stood. Probably not even within two hundred miles.

"You don't know what they put in those things. Some of it's toxic, too."

Charley didn't want to talk about garbage problems.

"Well, my nephew, Conrad, is opening a used car lot in Miles City next to his garage. He'd move his business to Dry Creek if he thought he could get enough customers. Talk to him and maybe he can put you in a newer car for reasonable payments."

"I'm certainly not going to start buying things on credit at this stage of my life," Edith said. She looked up at Charley. "You remember the problems we all had that year when hail destroyed the wheat crop and most of the men had to work in Billings over Christmas just to make ends meet?"

"I sure do," Charley said. "I know Harold went. I thought it must have been hard on him. He didn't talk much about it though when he came back."

Edith took a deep breath and looked down slightly. "He wasn't proud of everything he did that winter."

"Oh?"

"I don't suppose he told you about it?" Edith looked up again.

"Not much. He said he had dinner with Elmer a few times."

"I'd forgotten Elmer was there that winter, too."

Charley thought he saw a tear starting to form in Edith's eyes.

"Don't worry," he said as fast as he could. "I'll go check on the Morgan place and see if there are any chokecherries."

Edith turned and started walking back up the coulee. "I don't need any chokecherries this year. All that jelly isn't good for us anyway."

"But what are we going to put on your biscuits at the harvest dinner?" Charley said as he took a couple of quick steps to bring himself even with Edith. He reached out and took her elbow without asking. The woman shouldn't be walking these coulees without even a stick to balance herself.

"There's no need for me to make any biscuits," Edith said and he heard her take another quick breath. "Not when we don't have the jelly."

"Oh, boy," Charley said. He was in trouble now. All of the men he sat with around that old woodstove looked forward to Edith's biscuits as much as her jelly. They claimed they were the lightest, fluffiest biscuits they'd ever eaten. Charley figured he'd have to drink his coffee at home until spring if he didn't get some chokecherries.

He couldn't help but notice that Edith was upset about something. She'd let him take her elbow and help her on the climb, but she kept her arm stiff, as if she didn't want his help even though she knew she needed it.

It must be the chokecherries, Charley finally

decided. She kept saying she didn't need any berries and she wouldn't make any jelly this year. But she didn't speak with the free and easy style she usually had when she talked to him.

Charley suddenly realized what was going on. Edith was being polite to him.

"I'm sorry," Charley repeated softly for lack of anything better to say. He'd already apologized three times in as many minutes, but he would do it again if it would make Edith talk to him like she used to. It made him feel lonesome, her being so polite.

Edith waved his words away. Charley wasn't sure if that meant she'd already forgiven him or that there was no way she'd ever forgive him. They finished the walk up the coulee in silence.

They reached their vehicles at the top of the incline before Charley got a good clear look at Edith.

"What'd you do to your hair?"

"It's just falling down," she said, lifting a hand to her neck. "Doris June was going to cut it, but we decided not to."

"Oh, well, it looks nice."

Edith didn't answer.

"I'll wait to see that you get it started," Charley said as they reached the door of Edith's car.

"Thank you," Edith said as she slid under the steering wheel of her car. Charley closed the car door for her.

"It should start fine," Edith said as she rolled down her window. "I took the car out and let the battery recharge after Pastor Matthew helped me with it yesterday."

Charley grunted.

"He said I should get a new battery. Maybe your nephew has a used one."

"He sells used cars, not used batteries. No one buys a used battery. That's something that needs to work right in a car."

"Well, Pastor Matthew fixed mine."

"Temporarily," Charley said as he started to walk toward his pickup.

"It's fine right now," he heard her say.

Charley climbed in his truck before Edith had a chance tell him that he didn't need to coast along behind her. He felt protective of her and that was just the way it was. He'd started feeling that way even before Harold had died.

Charley's wife Sue had started it all, asking him one day if he thought Edith hadn't looked a little sad the last time they'd seen her. His wife had assumed the Hargroves had been arguing and she'd asked him to talk some sense to Harold. Not that Charley ever did. He'd given Harold every chance to talk to him about any problems, but the man kept quiet. The only thing Charley had known to do was to suggest his wife invite Edith over to visit more often.

Charley wondered what his wife would think if she could see Edith now, driving so slowly and deliberately down the gravel road leading back to Dry Creek.

Now, of course, no one—probably not even Edith—remembered those days when she'd seemed so vulnerable. Both Sue and Harold were dead. But that left Charley. He knew. Everyone, including Edith, might think she was well able to take care of herself, but he knew better. Sometimes she needed help, just like everyone else.

Charley looked down at his gas gauge. He was going to need to keep his tank full if he intended to continue following her car around like the fool that he was.

Chapter Three

Edith had forgotten all about Elmer. Her hands were gripping the steering wheel of her car and it had nothing to do with driving down the gravel road. Until Charley had mentioned him, Edith had completely overlooked the fact that Elmer had been in Billings that winter, too. When Harold had assured her that he hadn't told anyone about Jasmine, she hadn't thought to ask if anyone had *seen* him with Jasmine. Like maybe Elmer.

There had been another man from Dry Creek in Billings that winter, too, but he'd moved his family away the following spring. They hadn't lived in Dry Creek long and they'd moved south to Tennessee shortly after that hard winter. His name had been William something. She thought it was William Townsend.

Edith looked out the rearview mirror and saw Charley faithfully following behind her in his pickup. She almost wished Charley had known about Harold's affair so she could ask his advice about what to do now.

It didn't seem right to just announce the affair now that Harold wasn't even alive to defend himself. And, after all these years, she wondered if there was any point to making it public. Maybe all it would do was shatter Doris June's heart.

But on the other hand, maybe the reason Jasmine contacted her was because she was planning to tell people what had happened. Edith watched enough daytime television to know people like that existed. She would rather the story came from her mouth than Jasmine's.

She just didn't know what to do.

Edith could see why people who tried to cover up things almost always got caught, assuming they didn't have a heart attack from the stress first. It was too hard to remember everything. And to know what to do at every twist and turn.

Edith arrived in Dry Creek and she honked her horn to signal Charley that she had made it back safely and that, while she'd appreciated his escort, she hadn't really needed it since her car had made it to town just fine. As usual.

In response, Charley rolled down his window and put his arm out to point at the café.

Edith smiled. Now that he'd shaved his moustache, her world had settled back into place. She had to admit she could use a cup of tea. It was the middle of the morning and she'd like nothing better than to sit with Charley and try to think of a way to get his advice without telling him anything he didn't already know.

Charley pulled up beside her car and was at her door to open it before she could get her hat pulled off.

She reached up to anchor the pins in her hair better as she looked at Charley.

"You could have gone ahead of me," Edith said as she finished with her hair. "There was no need to wait."

Charley grunted. "I won't always be there following behind you and what then? That's when your car's going to break down."

Edith swung her legs around to get out of the car. "Any car can go bad at any time."

"That's why you shouldn't be driving by yourself," Charley said triumphantly as he held out his hand to help her stand.

Edith took his hand graciously. "If my car breaks down, I'll just get someone to fix it. You don't need to worry."

Charley snorted, but he didn't say anything else as they walked toward the door of the Dry Creek Café. Linda Enger, the owner of the café, had put a sign over her small restaurant a few months ago. The café had a fifties look to it, with black-and-white linoleum on the floor and memorabilia hanging on the walls. She even displayed a guitar that belonged to her new husband, singing legend Duane Enger. He went on tour periodically and Linda loved to boast about where he was playing.

Edith could hear someone in the kitchen when they entered the café, but there were no other customers. She was glad for that just in case her conversation with Charley got more candid than she planned.

"How about here?" Charley asked as he led her to a table by the far wall.

Edith nodded.

There were two menus on the table, standing upright between the napkin holder and the salt and pepper shakers, but no one in Dry Creek ever looked at them. Everyone knew the regular items and if there was something special on the menu, Linda would let them know.

Linda brought out coffee for Charley and tea for Edith before she even asked what they wanted.

"Maybe some buttered toast," Edith said when Linda took their order.

"Biscuits for me if you have any," Charley added.

Linda went back to the kitchen.

Edith curved her hands around the hot cup. "I'm glad you wanted to stop. I've been meaning to ask you something."

"Yeah?"

Edith nodded and took a deep breath. "I've been wondering what you think about digging up old troubles."

"You mean like debts that aren't paid?"

"No, things that people did that were wrong, but happened a long time ago. Is there any reason to talk about it now?"

Charley looked a little surprised. "I don't know. I'd say it depends. Was anyone hurt?"

Edith nodded. "But it was a family matter."

Charley took a sip of his coffee. "Well, maybe it needs to be talked about in the family then."

"Oh, I don't know if there's any point to that. Doris June doesn't even—" Edith stopped. She hadn't meant to tell Charley it was *her* family she was discussing.

"Well," Charley said, clearing his throat. "I know Doris June loves you and she'd probably forgive you anything. Is this something you did as a mother when she was little?"

"Of course not, I was a good mother."

"I'm sure you were. I can't think of what else would be worth discussing at this stage of things though."

Edith could see she wouldn't get any good advice out of Charley this way. He couldn't help her unless she told him everything. She took a deep breath and looked over to be sure the kitchen door was still closed. "It was about Harold." She leaned over the table and whispered, "He had an affair."

"He *what?*" Charley had started to lift his cup for another sip, but he put it back down and coffee sloshed over the saucer. *"Harold?"*

Edith nodded. "And I'm not sure, but Elmer might know about it."

"Elmer, too?"

"Well, I don't know that Elmer was having an affair. I just know that Harold had one that winter in Billings."

"Ah," Charley said as he mopped up the coffee with his napkin. "I thought something was different with him when he came back."

Edith felt relieved. After all these years, the secret was out. She'd told someone besides that pastor who had died years ago. And, Charley hadn't looked at her in horror. He'd been surprised, yes, but he didn't look as if he was sitting there asking himself what she'd done wrong to drive Harold into the arms of another woman.

"Her name was Jasmine," Edith said.

"Never heard of her," Charley replied as he picked up his coffee cup again.

"She wants to meet me," Edith added.

"What?" Charley set his cup down again without taking a drink.

"Well, not really me. She wrote to Harold asking to talk to him and, since he's dead, I said I'd—"

"I can't think of what she can say now to make what happened back then better," Charley said. A muscle twitched along his jaw. "Hasn't she done enough damage?"

Edith felt warmed by his indignation on her behalf. She never lacked for a champion when Charley was around.

"I keep wondering if maybe she wants to apologize or something."

Charley just stared at her. "After all these years?"

Edith shrugged. "They have all kinds of programs where people apologize for things they did in the past, like in Alcoholics Anonymous. The more I think about it, the more I think that has to be it."

Edith looked at Charley. In those early years on the farm, she had always thought Charley had an average face. Her Harold had been the handsomest man around Dry Creek, with his thick black hair and clear blue eyes. In contrast, Charley had looked very ordinary with his sandy hair and moss-green eyes. Even if he had a moustache, a woman's gaze would slide right over Charley in a crowd. But that's because, Edith realized, most people didn't look at the bones in his face. Charley's whole face showed his strength. His jaw was firm. His cheekbones were set high. His hair was graying now, but he was clearly ready to take her part in any trouble she had.

"You're a good friend," Edith said. "A good friend."

* * *

Charley knew he should smile. He forced his lips into making an attempt. It was a sad day though when a woman looked at him as directly as Edith had and all she had in mind was friendship.

"We go back a long way," Charley said.

He wondered how Edith could still be so in love with Harold after all the man had done. It was true he had been a charmer, but he'd been gone a long time. Charley finally understood why she had been unhappy in those days long ago. She'd never said anything to his wife; he was sure of that. But she'd no doubt been miserable. How could Edith have been so loyal to a man who was unfaithful to her?

It was because she was a saint, Charley decided. Harold hadn't deserved her, that much was certain. Here she was still trying to protect his memory. If Harold were alive, Charley would have had some words with him behind a barn somewhere.

Not that it would help the woman sitting across the table from him.

"If I can do anything," Charley said.

Edith nodded. "I'm just a little worried about Elmer."

"I could talk to Elmer if you want. He's got a big mouth, but he wouldn't say anything to hurt you." *Especially if it was pointed out to him that there would be consequences.*

"If you can do it without telling him anything. I mean, just in case he doesn't know."

Charley nodded. "Leave it to me."

"You're a good—"

"Not a problem," Charley interrupted. He didn't

want to hear once again that he was a good friend. He'd been trying for months to find a way to be more than a friend to Edith. He'd even stopped going by her place at mealtimes, not wanting her to think he was only interested in her cooking. His wife had told him that Harold used to say he'd married Edith for her cooking. Charley didn't want to make that mistake—no woman should be told that.

Not that Charley had a list of romantic things to say instead. Of course, he'd done all he could to show he cared about the car she drove. And he was getting her some chokecherries. So far, though, neither of those things had made her look at him any differently. He couldn't be doing worse if he tried.

"Is there anything else I can do?" he asked.

Charley saw the hesitation on Edith's face.

"Anything," he repeated. He wasn't opposed to facing down someone besides Elmer if there was anyone else she was worried about.

Edith was silent for a moment. "You could help me look right."

Charley looked at her. That floppy hat of hers had left a red crease across her forehead after she took it off. Her hair was twisted in some way he didn't understand. Her face was pink with embarrassment. "You look fine."

"I don't mean *now*," Edith said. "I mean when I meet *her*."

"Oh."

"I've always thought she must have been beautiful."

Charley was almost wishing there was someone he could beat up for her. He hated to see her looking so vulnerable again. "She couldn't have been more beautiful than you."

That surprised her and then made her frown.

"I'm not asking for a boost to my morale. I want some real help," she said.

"Shouldn't Doris June give you that kind of advice?" Charley thought his neck might be sweating.

The kitchen door opened and Charley had never been so happy to see Linda, and that included the time he'd been up all night taking care of a sick horse and Linda was bringing him the first food he'd seen in twenty-some hours.

"Toast," Linda announced as she put the plate in front of Edith.

"And biscuits," she said, setting the plate of biscuits in front of Charley.

"Now, does anyone need jelly?" Linda beamed at them.

"What kind of jelly do you have?" Charley asked. He knew she had over a dozen flavors and he was happy to have her slowly list them all to him. Charley asked for the last flavor, orange marmalade, simply because it was the last flavor she mentioned and he needed some time to gather himself.

"See?" Edith said when Linda went back to the kitchen to get the jelly.

"What?"

"See how many kinds of jelly there are in this world? We don't need chokecherry. We can have grape."

"I'm going to get you those chokecherries," Charley said. "Just give me a little time. I haven't even had a chance to drive out to the Morgan place."

"I don't want to be a bother."

Charley grunted. "Then get your jars ready to make jelly."

Maybe making jelly would get Edith's mind off this Jasmine woman. At least, he hoped so.

Chapter Four

The next morning, Charley went by the hardware store as he usually did. Elmer didn't show up at his regular time, so Charley decided to go over to the church for a bit. He told himself he was only going there so he could finally move those old hymnals from the back Sunday school room to the shelves by the pastor's office. He'd meant to do it yesterday, but his morning had been spent with Edith and it took most of his afternoon to get her enough chokecherries from that coulee out by the Morgan place.

Charley was a little nervous about going to the church when no one but the pastor was there. He'd never been one of those people who felt the need to have pastoral counseling about everything they did in life and he wasn't going to become one now. If he happened to run into Pastor Matthew while he was at the church, though, and they just happened to have a conversation, that would be okay.

Charley felt a man should know his own mind

without having to talk with someone else. Still, he needed to move those hymnals and the bookshelf *was* just outside the pastor's office.

Charley didn't want to disturb Pastor Matthew, of course. That's why he carefully held the hymnals so they wouldn't fall to the floor and startle the pastor. If the pastor happened to look up and see him walking past though, no one could count that as an interruption.

"Charley," Pastor Matthew called out as Charley walked past the open doorway. "I've been meaning to check with you. Did you catch up with Mrs. Hargrove yesterday? How's her car running?"

Charley told himself it was only polite to turn back and stand in the open doorway to answer the pastor. No one liked to have to yell back and forth to have a conversation. "I sure did. She was out trying to get some chokecherries."

"She makes a good jelly. I always look forward to the jar she brings us at Christmas. Glory uses it to make thumbprint cookies. They're the twins' favorite."

Charley swallowed. He hadn't even known about the cookies. "I ended up getting the last of the choke-cherries at the Morgan place. There weren't many, but I found enough."

"That's good. The harvest dinner is coming up and her biscuits and jelly are the hit of the evening."

Charley shifted his weight so he stood up a little straighter. "The jelly will be there. I think she's going to make it tomorrow."

The two men were silent for a moment as Charley tried to think of a way to begin to talk about his problem. He almost wished he had a spiritual crisis—

that would be easier to talk about than what he had troubling him.

"How's your grandson doing? He getting along okay with Doris June?" the pastor finally asked.

Charley stepped inside the pastor's office.

"He worships her. She makes him those sour-cream raisin cookies that Edith makes. Doris June is pretty near as good a cook as her mother."

It was silent for another minute before Charley cleared his throat. "Speaking of Edith—I—ah—"

Charley couldn't think of how to say it so he just stopped.

"She's a fine woman," the pastor prodded. "Not perfect, of course, but—"

"She's closer to perfect than any woman I know," Charley snapped. He decided next time he wanted to talk he'd go into Miles City and see that dentist who didn't believe in using Novocain. "Just because a woman has a few opinions and doesn't know anything about cars doesn't mean she's not, well, perfect."

The pastor nodded.

Charley nodded back. He was glad they had that settled.

Charley was starting to turn to the door when the pastor said, "The two of you have been friends for a lot of years."

Charley turned back. "That's it right there."

The pastor frowned. "It's good to have friends, isn't it?"

"I don't want to be friends anymore." Charley spit it out and then took a breath.

Pastor Matthew looked bewildered. "Did you have

an argument? I hope I wasn't responsible. I truly thought someone should help her with her battery. She was trying to jump-start her car using the motor on her lawn mower."

"Well, that would never work."

"I know, that's why…" he trailed off. "Please, don't be upset with her about what I did."

"I'm not upset with her," Charley said. "I'm—I'm…"

For the life of him, Charley couldn't say he wanted to have a romantic relationship with Edith. In his own defense, though, he did have to say that the dentist in Miles City would have guessed the truth of everything by now. Of course, that man dealt all day long with people in pain who couldn't talk so he was good at understanding the unspoken agony in a man's eyes.

"Well, don't give up on your friendship," Pastor Matthew finally said. "I know all of us are a little annoying at times. But you and Mrs. Hargrove have been friends almost your whole lives. You don't just throw that kind of friendship away." The pastor stopped as though something had just occurred to him. "She's not mad at you, is she? I know she's awfully protective of that car of hers. Maybe you shouldn't have told her to get a new one."

"She only likes that car because Harold bought it."

The pastor nodded. "I'm sure the two of you will work things out. Just be patient with one another. Who knows? If you give her some time, she might even buy a different car."

Charley doubted that, but he nodded anyway. He sure wasn't going to reveal that it wasn't the car that was bothering him. It was that Edith kept that beat-up old vehicle like a shrine to her dead husband. And she knew all along that the man didn't deserve it. Harold had betrayed her. Most women he knew would have taken a hammer to that car years ago. All of which must have meant Edith had a powerful love for Harold that just wouldn't let go.

Charley hoped he lived long enough to see Edith give up that car. If she would even do that much, he would have reason to hope that she could break away from the past and begin a new future. He'd asked his nephew to give her a call and see if she was interested in a new car, but he told him not to expect to make a sale.

"Well, I better get the rest of these hymnals moved," Charley said as he started toward the door again.

"I'm glad you stopped by to talk," the pastor said.

"I wasn't really stopping to talk," Charley said as he stood in the door. "I was just moving the hymnals. If we don't move things around, we get in a rut."

The pastor nodded.

Charley left to stack the hymnals. He suddenly wished time would go back to last Sunday. Or better yet, two Sundays ago. That would be before Edith got the letter that had her so upset. And it would be well before she'd turned to him for beauty tips. *Him!* What kind of a man did she think he was? She wouldn't take car advice from him but she wanted to know what he thought about the way she looked?

Charley decided he was losing his touch with women. That was the only explanation.

Of course, he still had to help her. Maybe he should drive out to Elmer's place and try to talk to him there. It might be better than waiting for him to come to the hardware store anyway. He'd want to ask his questions in private, just in case Elmer did have anything interesting to say.

Elmer lived with his dog in the bunkhouse on his old ranch. When he'd retired, he'd leased the land out to the Elkton Ranch and, since his wife had died, he'd decided the main house was too big to clean and too hard to heat in the winter. Besides, Elmer, apart from that old Cadillac of his, was a simple man. The bunkhouse suited him fine.

Charley drove his pickup down the lane leading into the yard and parked it next to the Cadillac right in front of the bunkhouse. The dog started barking and Elmer came to stand in the doorway.

Charley reached over and picked up the pint jar of fresh-squeezed orange juice he'd gotten from the café on his way out of Dry Creek. He opened the door to his pickup and stepped down.

"Didn't see you this morning so I thought you might be sick. Brought you some orange juice," Charley said as he held up the jar.

"There was a day when you'd have brought me a bottle of whiskey if you thought I had a cold," Elmer grumbled.

Charley smiled. "Well, we've changed, haven't we?"

It seemed like a lifetime ago since he and Elmer were young and wild together. His wife's faith had brought Charley to the Lord when he was in his thirties and he'd never regretted giving up his old habits. He wasn't opposed to using the past to move Elmer into the right conversation, though.

"I bet the last time you really let loose was that

winter in Billings," Charley said as he handed the jar to Elmer. "Never did hear the stories of those days."

"Man, it was something else," Elmer said with a shake of his head.

"Oh?" Charley sat down on one of the wooden chairs that stood on the low porch to the bunkhouse.

Elmer followed him and eased himself into a chair as well. "We used to go to this place where they had wrestling. If you've never seen live wrestling, you're missing something."

"I thought you would be out painting the town red," Charley said. "You know, wine, women and song."

Elmer grinned. "I was a married man back then."

So was Harold Hargrove but that didn't stop him, Charley thought.

"You expect me to believe you all walked the straight and narrow?" Charley asked as casually as he could.

"What does it matter?" Elmer looked at him suspiciously. "It was a long time ago."

Charley nodded. He would bet money that Elmer knew some secrets from those days, but he wasn't going to give them up easily.

"Just curious, that's all," Charley said as he stood. "That car of Edith's had me thinking of Harold. I wondered what he'd say if he knew she was still driving it."

"He'd say she was one stubborn woman."

"Ever wonder if our wives would have kept one of our old cars like that?" Charley asked as he leaned on the post holding up the porch roof. "If we'd died before them, I mean."

Elmer snorted. "I know mine wouldn't. Not even

the Cadillac. She didn't have much sentiment in her, my wife."

"Well, life wasn't always easy for the women around here."

Elmer nodded. "Can't say I don't have some regrets when all is said and done. I wish I'd been better to her."

"Yeah," Charley said. He'd never cheated on his wife, but he wished he'd taken her on a few trips. She'd always wanted to go to Florida to see the alligators but he'd never taken her there. "Well, I better be going."

"Thanks for stopping by," Elmer said.

"Yeah. I'm glad you're not sick."

Elmer nodded and raised the jar of juice in a salute. "This will fight off anything that might come my way."

"See you tomorrow." Charley started walking to his pickup.

"I'll beat you at checkers."

Charley had opened his pickup door, but he turned around and grinned. "Not if I can help it."

The drive back to Dry Creek was too short. Charley kept thinking of the things he hadn't done that would have pleased his wife. Being a husband was something that took some doing and he wished he'd been better at it. Mostly, he'd just taken his wife for granted. She'd always been there. She was like the land in that way. The seasons came and went, some good and some bad, but a few things he could always count on. His God, his land and his wife.

The southeastern part of Montana grew strong farm wives. They knew how to love a man despite his failings.

Charley knew he had to report to Edith that he hadn't gotten anything useful out of his conversation with Elmer, but he thought he'd stop and have a cup of coffee at the hardware store first. He wanted to gather his thoughts and shake off his memories.

Chapter Five

Edith had the Mason jars stacked on her kitchen counter; they were drying after their first scalding. The boiling water had steamed up her house slightly and made her cheeks damp. She'd washed and sorted the chokecherries while the jars were boiling and she'd laid them on a towel to dry. She'd wait until tomorrow to crush the berries and make the jelly. She didn't like to rush things.

In the meantime, she'd started making a batch of yeast bread. She didn't often bake bread anymore, but there was nothing like a slice of fresh bread dipped in a bit of chokecherry syrup that hadn't yet had time to gel. She and Harold had almost made a ritual out of fresh bread and syrup on jelly-making day.

Edith heard the knock on her front door just as she finished setting the bread dough in her brown crockery bowl to rise. The letter was still in her apron pocket, but she hadn't worried about it as much since she'd told Charley all that had happened those many years ago. It was comforting to have a friend like him. She figured that was probably Charley at her door now.

Edith grabbed one of her white dish towels and wiped her hands as she walked across the living room to her front door. She could see the shape of a tall man through the frosted round window in her door.

"Oh." Edith opened the door and was surprised it wasn't Charley. The young man did look a little like him, though. "Hello."

"Hi, I'm—" The screen door stood between them. He was wearing a white shirt and a tie that seemed to be giving him some difficulty—he was running his finger around the inside of his shirt collar.

"Why, you're Charley's nephew. I recognize you now. You used to come visit him on the farm years ago."

"Yes, ma'am," he said with a smile. "I'm Conrad Nelson."

"Well, it's so good to see you. How've you been?"

The man nodded. "Pretty good. The reason I'm here is—well, my uncle thought you might be interested in some information on my cars. I know I should have called, but I wanted to drive down to Dry Creek today anyway and I thought I'd stop and tell you about the different used cars I have on my lot right now."

"I'm really not sure if—"

"No need to decide anything today," Conrad said smoothly. "You'll be wanting to see them for yourself, I'm sure. I've never known a woman yet who didn't want to look good in a new car."

For the first time it occurred to Edith that getting a new hairstyle might not be enough to make her feel comfortable talking to Jasmine Hunter. The other woman would not be driving a car that was thirty years old any more than she'd have her hair combed into the same old bun she'd worn for decades.

Edith opened the screen door and invited Charley's nephew inside.

Fifteen minutes later, she had her sweater on and she was walking out the front door with Conrad following behind.

"I'm not sure that it's the one that will suit you best," Conrad mumbled a little frantically as he followed her. "I only drove it down because it's not raining today."

Edith didn't pause as she walked down the steps of her porch. "Well, it has a lid, doesn't it?"

"Top. They call it a top."

"It doesn't rain that often here anyway," Edith said as she kept walking to the curb. She didn't mention that it snowed much more than it rained, but she figured that was a small detail. She didn't drive in the snow these days anyway.

"It's beautiful," Edith whispered, stopping short out of respect for the car that was in front of her. It looked like a bright cherry dropped in a bucket of sand. Edith looked up at the streetlight above the car to see where that shine was coming from. The light was off—it was the middle of the day. The car was shining all on its own.

The bright red convertible would do justice to someone like Marilyn Monroe—and Edith wanted it.

"My uncle thought you might like something in blue," Conrad stuttered as he came up to stand beside her. He was running his finger around his collar again. "I have a nice sedan in a light blue that came in a month ago. It's a nice conservative car."

Nice and conservative wouldn't impress anyone, Edith thought.

"How much is this one?" she asked as she pointed at the convertible.

Conrad swallowed. "Well, I have it marked for seventy-five hundred, but I guess if a person had a trade-in—"

"Oh." Edith stopped herself. She'd never thought about trading in *her* car. Her car was still, well, her car. She didn't like to think of someone else driving it.

"You'll want to think about it," Conrad said, sounding relieved.

"Of course, I just…"

Edith felt her shoulders slump.

"It wouldn't hurt to test-drive it though," Conrad said, rallying. "Then maybe you could mention to people that it runs good and, for a convertible, no one will find a better deal in this part of the state."

Edith eyed the car. "It would be nice to see how it runs."

Everyone had been telling her how much easier new cars were to drive and it would seem that a convertible would be one of the easiest since there was so little to it. If nothing else, she should try out the steering since the car was right here in front of her, practically begging to be driven down the street.

Charley thought he was hallucinating. He was sitting by the window of the Dry Creek Café, minding his own business and finishing his second cup of coffee. He was, of course, looking out the window at the one street that ran through Dry Creek. It was just habit to look in that direction, he never really expected to see anything more exciting than a dog trotting by.

Even after he saw Edith in that red convertible, he still couldn't believe it. So he stood up and went to the front door of the café, thinking that maybe the window had warped his vision and he wasn't really seeing that woman in that car.

He was barely in time to catch her taillights. Edith, who putted along in her old car like it was a golf cart, was driving the convertible like a jet coming in for a landing. Or a takeoff, he wasn't sure which.

He felt a headache coming on.

Whatever was happening, he figured he better get in his pickup and trail along behind Edith. A woman her age should have more sense. And, he had to admit, she usually did. That letter must have rattled her more than she had let on. He should have made more of an effort to dig the truth out of Elmer—he'd just have to get the job done. He'd seen Elmer's Cadillac go by so he knew the man was sitting at the hardware store by now. He'd go talk to him once Edith was safely back at her house.

Charley's pickup hiccupped in protest when he put it in gear. He knew how the vehicle felt. No one wanted to have to follow Edith when she was driving. It was a thankless job at best. She never appreciated it. But Charley wasn't looking for a Good Samaritan of the Year award. He watched over Edith to settle his own nerves, not hers.

Five miles down the road, Edith was trying to get more comfortable in the smooth leather seats. She had never felt the breeze in her hair like this—her pins had fallen loose at the outskirts of Dry Creek and she couldn't stop to fix them. Even in her sensible shoes, she had a hard time adjusting to the pedals and she'd mistakenly pressed down hard on the gas as she left town. Still, she thought she was doing quite well.

She looked in the rearview mirror and saw Charley charging after her in his pickup. She knew what he'd say—this wasn't the car for her. Well, she'd come to that same conclusion herself before she'd even left Dry Creek. But it didn't seem polite to return it to Conrad without spending enough time to make it look like she'd had some difficulty in making that decision.

She held her arm up high and waved to Charley. Now, that's something she couldn't do in her old car. She knew there was a farm road just ahead and she could use it to turn around easily. She'd be back in Dry Creek before she knew it.

Edith felt she'd adjusted to the pedals pretty well by the time she pulled back into town. She saw Conrad standing at the bottom of the steps to the hardware store just staring at the road in front of him. She honked the horn to let him know she was back. Then she honked it again because she liked the sound. She wondered if she could get a horn like that for her old car. Her car's horn sounded like a foghorn; the convertible's horn sounded more like a musical instrument in a symphony. Sometimes it was those small things that made a big difference.

Edith slowed the convertible to a stop in front of the hardware store. The horn must have attracted some interest, because several of the men had come out and were standing on the porch.

"I'm back," Edith announced as she turned off the car and pulled the key out of the ignition.

"Thank God," Conrad said as he walked up to car.

Edith noticed he looked a little pale. She was going to suggest he might try to get more iron in his diet when she noticed that the men were coming down the steps and heading to the car.

"Whooee," Fred Wagner said as he reached out to touch the fender. The Wagners had a farm north of Dry Creek. Fred had started the farm, but his sister's son worked it now.

"This is sure a sight," Elmer said, almost purring as he ran his hands over the hood. "What color is this anyway? Firebrick-red? It almost looks like there's some blue in it."

Edith had definitely found something that appealed to all men. She hadn't seen this much excitement about a vehicle since the owner of the Elkton Ranch bought that big combine and the delivery man had driven it right through town.

Just then Charley pulled up beside her and stepped out of his pickup.

"You could have been killed." Charley didn't even look at the car, he just glowered at her.

Edith decided maybe the convertible didn't appeal to all men.

Charley turned and faced his nephew. "I don't know what you were thinking! She's not—" Charley stopped and looked back at Edith.

"I'm perfectly able to drive a car," Edith said.

"I know," Charley said and his voice had quieted down. "It's just—"

Edith took pity on him. "I'm not buying the convertible."

Her announcement caused a few murmurs among the men.

"Well, if you're not buying it, I might then," Elmer said. "I'd have my convertible for summer and my Cadillac for the winter."

Charley snorted. "Neither one of those cars is worth anything in the snow."

"Well, maybe I'm not worried about driving them in the snow. Maybe I'm thinking of setting up a— what do you call it?—a collection. Yes, siree, I've always wanted a collection of cars like the rich folks have. Like the ones you see on television."

"You don't even have a garage to keep the cars," Charley pointed out. "They'll just sit out there and rust at your place."

Elmer's chin just went up in the air. "I can clean out my barn if I need storage."

"Fine."

Edith almost smiled. Charley was having a hard day. She did the only thing she could think of that would make him feel better. She handed the keys for the convertible back to Conrad.

Charley was right there to open the car door for her. He held out his hand and Edith was grateful for it. She didn't know why they had to make these convertibles so close to the ground. It was almost impossible for a lady in a dress to make a graceful exit without someone to help her.

Edith assured Conrad she would call him if she wanted to test drive another car and then she and Charley started walking back to her house.

Somehow in all of the confusion of saying goodbye to everyone at the hardware store, Charley had kept hold of the hand that he'd taken to help her out of the car. She didn't think he realized he still had it because he seemed preoccupied as they walked.

Edith felt her pulse beat a little faster. It wasn't every day she held a man's hand, even if it didn't mean anything. Still, Charley was a fine-looking man. Ever since she thought of Charley with his moustache, she was becoming more aware of the fact that any number of women would like to date him.

"Do you think Elmer will really buy that convertible?" Edith finally asked, a little breathlessly. She needed to stop thinking of Charley like that. He was her friend and nothing more. That's the way it had always been.

They were already halfway to her house.

Charley shrugged. "No telling. The man loves cars."

When they got to the walkway leading up to her house, Edith thought surely Charley would let go of her hand. But he swung back the gate with his left hand as they entered her yard and kept his right hand firmly attached to hers.

"I'm sorry I made you nervous with that convertible," Edith said as they walked up the steps to her porch. That was the only reason she could think of for Charley's strange behavior. "I really am fine when I'm driving though. You don't need to worry."

Charley turned and looked squarely at her. "I don't know what I'd do without you."

Edith felt a little flustered. "You're a good friend to me, too."

Charley grunted and finally released her hand, which was a good thing as they were in front of her door and she needed to turn the handle to open it.

"Would you like some coffee or something?"

Charley shook his head. "Thanks, but I need to go back and talk to Elmer."

"Maybe later then," Edith said as she twisted the doorknob and opened her door.

"Yeah," Charley said, heading back down the steps.

Edith stepped inside her living room, but she stood on the other side of the screen door and watched Charley as he made his way down her sidewalk. She doubted Charley was having the fluttery feelings she was, but something was different with him these days and she couldn't put her finger on it. He just wasn't as carefree as he used to be. She could tell by the slump in his shoulders that something was bothering him.

And, Edith asked herself, what kind of a friend was she to him? Here he was on his way to talk to Elmer on her behalf and she didn't even know what Charley's problem was. She hoped it wasn't discouragement about dating some woman, but if it was she needed to put aside her own feelings and talk to him. No one needed friends more than someone who was suffering from unhappiness in love. She, of all people, knew that.

She'd have to take him a plant, she told herself as she closed the door. And some fresh bread. She hadn't taken him a proper housewarming gift yet and she needed to do that. She should also write him a little note telling him how much she appreciated him. Sometimes a person needed to tell their friends how important they were to them.

Chapter Six

Charley was on his fifth game of checkers and he was thinking of letting Elmer beat him on this one. Maybe that would loosen the man's tongue. They were sitting in a corner of the hardware store and Charley had been doing his best to keep talking about flower seeds. If Elmer hadn't droned on about the different colors of blue a day ago, Charley would have felt like a fool.

As it was, Charley had summoned all of his creativity to mention jasmine seeds half a dozen times. It was hard to make it sound natural, especially since he didn't even know if jasmine grew from a seed. Maybe it was a bulb. So far, Elmer had flushed every time Charley mentioned the word *jasmine,* but he still didn't own up to knowing anything.

Charley decided he needed to step it up. "Ever notice how women like to name their baby girls after flowers?"

Elmer grunted.

"I've met a lot of Roses in my day," Charley continued. "And a Lilly or two. Can't say that I've come across any babies by the name of Jasmine though. How about you?"

"Me?" Elmer looked up from the board in surprise. "I don't know anything about naming babies."

"Sorry," Charley said. He'd mangled that one. Everyone in Dry Creek knew that the sadness of the Maynard marriage had been that they'd had no children. Elmer's wife had longed for a child until the day she died.

"King me," Elmer said as he moved one of his black pieces to the edge of the board.

"Of course."

Charley doubled Elmer's playing piece.

"I did know a Jasmine once," Elmer finally said softly as he captured one of Charley's pieces. "She was a beauty."

Charley froze. "In Billings?"

Elmer nodded. "It was a long time ago."

"Did Harold know you knew her?"

Elmer's head came up at that. "Harold? What's it got to do with Harold?"

"I don't know," Charley said. Which was the truest statement he'd made all day.

"Did Harold say something about me and Jasmine to you?"

Charley shook his head. "No, he never mentioned anything about Jasmine to me."

Elmer looked at him suspiciously. "I'm not proud of it, you know."

"No one ever is."

To Charley's surprise, he didn't need to let Elmer win this game. He did it without Charley even noticing.

* * *

Edith couldn't think in her kitchen. The steam from boiling the jars still lingered in the air and the smell of yeast from the bread was distracting. She had pulled out a tablet and was trying to write an encouraging note to Charley. She couldn't think of the right words to say, though. She wanted him to know that she was on his side no matter what his problem was, but he hadn't admitted to her that he had a problem so she didn't want to mention anything. Which made it very hard to write something.

Finally, she decided that what she needed was a greeting card. That way she didn't have to think of anything to say herself. She could just sign her name and Charley would know that she cared about him and was grateful for his friendship because the card would have the words right there in black and white. Unfortunately, the only cards she had at the moment were birthday cards and those would never work.

It took her a minute to remember that the pastor had a whole box of different kinds of cards. He mailed them to people in the church who had done something helpful during the week or were having a hard time. She was sure he would let her buy one of the cards to send to Charley.

It was the middle of the afternoon before Edith started walking over to the church. She'd had to wait for the bread to come out of the oven. Then she'd rubbed a generous bit of butter on the hot loaves before they cooled on their racks and that took a few more minutes as well. Eventually, though, she was ready to go.

The sky had grown overcast in the past hour and Edith decided it was good that she had taken her ride in the convertible this morning. Speaking of which, she noticed that the car was parked over at the café—Conrad must still be in town. She wondered if he'd looked out the café window lately to see that rain clouds were gathering.

Edith never could ignore someone in need so, instead of just walking by the café, she stepped up on the porch and opened the café door. Sure enough, Conrad was sitting at a table by the new jukebox. He'd taken his tie off and it was lying on the table beside an empty plate that had been pushed to the side. He had a notebook in front of him and he looked like a man deep in some kind of thought.

"It looks like it might rain," Edith announced from the doorway. Conrad was the only customer in the café. It sounded like Linda was in the kitchen. "Just thought you should know."

Conrad stood up, looking alarmed. "But it can't rain. Elmer isn't back yet."

"It's cloudy."

Conrad quickly walked over to the window and bent down so he could see the sky without any interference from the roof over the porch. "How long does it take him to drive to where he lives and back here, anyway?"

"Maybe twenty minutes."

Conrad ran his fingers through his hair. "He's been gone an hour. He was supposed to bring me one of his old pickups as part of the down payment on the convertible."

"Well, then," Edith said. Elmer had been trying to trade a couple of those pickups off for decades. "That explains it. None of his old pickups run very well. He probably can't get any of them started."

Edith hoped Charley never compared her car with Elmer's pickups. They were all old vehicles, but she—unlike Elmer—kept hers in running condition. Something did not need to be useless just because it was old. Of course, it might need more attention, but that was to be expected.

"But I need to get back to Miles City," Conrad said. "I only agreed to accept an old pickup because I thought he'd be back soon."

"Hmm." Edith could see the boy was distressed. "If you give me time to step over to the church, I could drive you to Miles City. Of course, we'd need to put the lid on Elmer's convertible."

"Top. It's called a top. And I don't think my uncle would like me to ask you to take me into Miles City."

"Well, you didn't ask. I offered."

Edith wondered if she should add a line in her card to Charley encouraging him to get over his worry about her and her car.

"I certainly am going to need a ride if Elmer doesn't show up here pretty soon," Conrad said slowly. "Uncle Charley can't expect me to walk all the way back."

Edith smiled. It did her heart good to hear someone call Charley "uncle." She'd always wished she'd had some nieces and nephews. It hadn't worked out that way though and she'd been grateful she at least had Doris June. And now she had a grandson in Brad, Curt's son. She was blessed.

"I hope you do move your business to Dry Creek," Edith said. It would be good for Charley to have more family around. Maybe then he wouldn't feel so down about whatever was bothering him.

"I'm trying to figure out how I can do that," Conrad admitted. "I've been working on a business plan. The garage is the big part of my business. The used cars are just a sideline, but maybe that could change."

Edith nodded. "We're always on the lookout for more new businesses. We might even be giving away free space for a year. We did that when the bakery started up. Did Charley ever mention the woman who started it? Lizette Baker? She had a dance studio, too. Of course, she didn't last long, not after she married Judd Bowman. She pretty much closed down everything when she had the baby, although she still bakes donuts if people order them directly from her."

"You don't need to worry about me getting married," Conrad said with a grin. "I've pretty much sworn off women."

"Oh, no, that's too bad," Edith said. "A young man like you should be married."

Conrad laughed and he sounded just like Charley, Edith noticed. "I should be rich, too, but I'm not."

Edith shook her head and assured Conrad she would be back soon. She never would get used to how set on staying single some young people were these days. When she was their age, it seemed like everyone got married. It was what defined a person as an adult.

On the whole, though, she wasn't sure that had been a good way to do things either. Even with all of her troubles, she was glad she'd gotten married because she had Doris June. But not all couples had children. She wondered if she'd be happy that she'd gotten married if she and Harold had been childless. She thought on it as she walked over to the church, but she just couldn't decide. She supposed there was good to both the married and the single life.

The wrought-iron rails on the steps leading up to the church were cold when Edith touched them. She thought they might be a little damp, too, as though the air was gathering moisture for a thunderstorm.

The late afternoon sun didn't spill into the church today like it sometimes did. Edith would have thought the place was deserted if she hadn't heard the soft sound of a radio being played somewhere. It was probably coming from the pastor's office, because the door was open.

"Pastor Matthew," Edith called out as she walked toward the office. She figured the door being open was an invitation to come in, but she didn't want to sneak up on the man anyway.

She could hear the echo of her hard-soled shoes as she walked across the tile floor. The main part of the church was carpeted, but the entry hall and a strip along the back of the sanctuary was tile. With snow and rain, it had been hard to keep the carpet clean in this area and the women's group had tiled the back section last year.

Pastor Matthew was expecting her by the time Edith reached his office door.

"Mrs. Hargrove," the pastor said as he stood up and smiled at her. "What a pleasure. Come in. Would you like some tea? I have hot water going in the kitchen."

"No, I'm fine," Edith said as she reached into the pocket of her sweater and took out her folded dollar bill. "I won't be staying. I just wanted to know if I could buy one of those cards from you. You know, the ones to send to people in the church?"

"Well, sure," Pastor Matthew said as he sat back down at his desk and opened a drawer. "Who's it for? Doris June? I have some nice flowered ones."

Edith shook her head. "No, it's Charley."

"Ahhh," Pastor Matthew said as he pulled a square box from the drawer. "I have some nice cards here someplace. What are you looking for? Housewarming? Something like 'welcome to the neighborhood'?"

Edith frowned. If she'd known what she wanted to say to Charley, she wouldn't need a card. "No, not exactly. I've got a plant for that."

Pastor Matthew nodded. "A plant says it all." He kept flipping through the box of cards. "I have one here with a tractor on the front. It says something about retiring."

"Oh, no, that won't do."

The pastor looked up. "I do have some blank cards at the back."

Edith shook her head. The whole point of getting a card was to have words written on it already. "I don't suppose any of those cards talk about friendship?"

"Of course," the pastor said.

Edith noticed the pastor looked a little happier than before. There was a smile in his eyes.

"I'm always happy to see people in the family mend their relationships with each other," the pastor said as he triumphantly lifted up a card. "This one is perfect for that."

"Oh, we don't need anything mended. It's not that kind of a card. It's more of an appreciation card."

"Oh," the pastor said, putting one card back in the

box and looking down at the other. "I think that just leaves the flowered ones."

"Well, surely men appreciate each other," Edith said as she walked closer to the deck and looked down at the cards. "They shouldn't all be flowers."

Pastor Matthew shrugged. "Men just don't send men cards about that kind of thing, I guess."

Edith ended up with a card of pansies. It was the best she could do. Charley had helped her with the pansy baskets for church last Mother's Day so at least he would have some connection to the card. Those baskets had been one more thing he'd done for her, come to think of it.

She handed her dollar to the pastor and slipped the card into the pocket of her loose cardigan sweater.

"I hope you…ah, enjoy the card," the pastor said. He looked her in the eye. "And that everything's okay between you and Charley."

"Of course it's okay."

The pastor nodded. "That's good, because the two of you have been good friends for too long to let anything come between you." He hesitated. "If you ever need to talk about it, just let me know."

Edith nodded as she turned toward the door. "I will."

Of course she wouldn't. But she doubted there would ever be a need. Even with the fluttery feelings she'd had lately when she was around Charley, the two of them had one of the most uncomplicated relationships she could imagine between a man and a woman. She wondered for a moment if she should write that in the card, but then she decided against it. Somehow she didn't think it would look so good in black and white. He might decide she thought *he* was uncomplicated. She wasn't sure a man would like to hear that any more than a woman would.

Besides, it wasn't true. Charley might appear uncomplicated at first glance, but when a person got to know him better he was really quite complex.

When Edith walked out of the church, a raindrop fell on her head. She looked up and saw that the sky had gotten even grayer while she was inside picking out her card. She pushed the card deeper into the pocket of her sweater so it would stay dry. Then she hurried down the steps and started over to the café. Fortunately, Conrad had put the lid on that car. She hoped it didn't leak.

Edith wrapped the sweater more closely around herself as she walked. At least she didn't have to worry about the rain ruining her hairstyle. Maybe that's why she'd worn her hair in a bun all those years. A woman didn't have to constantly fix her hair when it was all pulled back like that. If she got the hairpins in right, she was set for the day.

By the time Edith reached the porch of the café, it was raining steadily. She opened up the door and noticed that several people had come inside, probably to keep dry. Linda's sister Lucy was there and Lance, one of the hands at the Elkton Ranch, was leaning against the counter and having a cup of coffee.

She found Conrad sitting at the same table he'd been using earlier.

"If you need me to drive you, we'd better start now. I think I'll be fine in rain, but if it turns to hail, I can't say for sure."

Conrad shook his head. "Thanks, but Uncle Charley just called over here and he said I should spend the night with him. He's on his way here now."

Edith frowned slightly. "Did you tell him I'd offered to drive you home?"

Conrad nodded. "Don't think he thought much of that idea."

"No, I suppose not." Edith decided maybe she should say something in her card about the driving after all. Charley couldn't expect her to stop driving places just because he was worried. Of course, Miles City was pretty far and it would have been dark before she got back. She would be having second thoughts about driving there even without Charley's objections.

Edith walked over to a table by the window. The rain was hitting the glass sideways and streaking down the window.

As she sat there, she decided she just didn't like having a man put arbitrary limits on her. It reminded her too much of having a husband. Harold had never worried about her like Charley did, but he still managed to keep her close to the farm with one excuse or another.

"Tea?" Linda asked as she came by the table with a pot of hot water.

"Please."

Edith watched Linda pour the water into the cup. Then Edith picked out a lemon tea bag from the small basket in the middle of the table.

She didn't know why she was thinking so much about her marriage lately. She'd been pondering it even before she got that letter. And the suggestion that

Charley might be dating someone didn't help. It was only natural to think of how many changes there were when people got married.

Her life had been very different when she'd been married to Harold. She kept that mustard-colored car to remind her of her past. Harold had bought the car twenty-some years ago. It had been a completely selfish purchase on his part—he hadn't even pretended otherwise. It was *his* car. She wasn't to drive it.

After Harold died, it had taken her months to get behind the wheel of the thing. She'd been used to taking the farm pickup if she needed to go someplace so she continued doing that. And then one day she hung the locket Harold had given her on the rearview mirror in the car and decided Harold would not rule her life anymore. She took her heart back completely from the man when she turned the key in the ignition.

Ever since then she had driven his car. It had started out as a defiant gesture, but over the years, she had formed her own bond with the car. She felt as if it knew where she had been in her life and it comforted her to drive it.

Edith took the tea bag out of her cup and sighed. She really didn't want to break in a new car.

A few minutes later, Charley came into the café, shaking rain off his hat. He wore a beige jacket.

"It's a downpour out there," Charley announced as he looked around. He smiled when he saw Edith and walked over to her table. "I'm glad you didn't try to drive into Miles City."

"Well, it is pretty wet," Edith conceded. She had already finished her tea so she started to stand.

"You just finishing?"

Edith nodded. "I should be getting home."

Charley looked around. "Let me see if I can borrow an umbrella from Linda. I'll walk you so you don't get soaked."

"That would be nice." Edith remembered the appreciation card she had in the pocket of her sweater. She wouldn't want that to get wet. Not when Charley was just giving her another reason to send it.

Charley went to talk to Linda and came back with a large, black umbrella.

"Ready?" Charley asked.

Edith nodded as she pulled the collar up on her sweater.

Charley opened the door. The porch had a roof of sorts so they stood there for a moment while Charley opened the umbrella. The sky was completely gray.

The rain started to beat on the umbrella as soon as the two of them walked down the steps. A few seconds later, a stream of water started flowing off the corner of the umbrella that was directly above Charley's hat.

"You can move the umbrella over to cover you, too," Edith said. "I won't melt."

"I'm fine," Charley said. "That's why I wear my hat in the rain."

Edith couldn't remember the last time she'd walked in the rain with a man. They walked close together because of the umbrella and she felt sheltered. Charley insisted she take his arm as they walked across the wet asphalt between the café and her house. She could feel the dampness of the air on the back of her neck. She felt her pocket to be sure the card there was keeping dry.

"I hope Elmer enjoys his convertible," Edith said as they neared her house. She always liked the smell of wet wool and a man's aftershave lotion—it was the simple things, of course. She hoped Charley didn't think he needed to dress himself up too much if he did decide to date.

Charley grunted. "I'm just glad you didn't buy it."

"I wouldn't have a place to keep it anyway," Edith said as Charley opened the gate to her yard. "I put my car in the garage so the convertible would need to be on the street."

Charley frowned down at her. Rain streamed off the back of his hat and just missed his neck. "I can't believe you'd put the convertible on the street and keep that old car of yours in the garage."

Edith shrugged. "That old car has some good years left in her."

Charley didn't say anything. He shifted the umbrella so it would keep her dry as they climbed the steps to her porch. When they stood under the roof of her porch, Charley brought the umbrella down and shook it a little before pushing the button to collapse it.

Then he turned to her. "If it's a matter of money, I have some put aside. I could get you a newer car."

Edith blinked. "I can't let you do that."

"Why not?"

"Well, because—" Edith sputtered to a stop. Even with the sweater she wore, her neck was cold and she shivered a bit. "What would people say?"

Charley smiled, reaching over to straighten the collar on her sweater. "They'd say you had a friend."

"Well, I know you've been a good friend, but—" Edith couldn't think. It just wasn't done.

"We all help each other around here," Charley said. "You know that."

"Yes, but this isn't lending me a cup of sugar. Or picking me those chokecherries. I have a little saved up for repairs on the car, but a new car—I wouldn't be able to repay you."

"I'm not asking you to," Charley said as he opened her door. "Why don't you go on in and get out of the cold."

Edith was over the threshold when she turned. "Want to come in?"

"I better get back to Conrad," Charley said. "We'll talk tomorrow."

She nodded and watched Charley walk down her sidewalk. Suddenly, the appreciation card in her sweater pocket didn't seem nearly large enough. She couldn't accept his offer of a new car, of course—especially since she really didn't want a new car—but she was still astonished that he had offered to buy her one.

Edith kept her eyes on Charley until he went back into the café. Then she turned from the door and switched the overhead light on in her living room. With the sky so gray, she couldn't tell if dusk were here or not. But the room would have been filled with shadows if she didn't have the light on. Edith closed her door and sat down on the sofa.

She sat there for a long minute.

She didn't know what to make of Charley's offer. Of course, she knew they were good friends. If Charley discovered that he needed an operation, she would give him all of the money she had if that would help.

But a new car for her wasn't a life-and-death matter. It wasn't a cause for the benevolence fund of the church or something for the community to pass the hat over. She was fine with that old mustard-colored car. Granted, the vehicle no doubt needed some work done to it, but she would see to that when she had to.

The air in the house still smelled like bread and it was a little chilly. Edith turned on her furnace and walked into the kitchen. She pulled the card out of her sweater pocket and put it on the kitchen table. She needed to think about what to say to Charley in addition to the words already printed on the card which she decided wouldn't be enough. Maybe there was a good scripture verse she could use to help make her point.

She sat down at the table and brushed her hands over the lavender envelope that matched the pansy card. It was a little damp so she got a thick cookbook from the cupboard and set it on top of the envelope. She didn't want it to wrinkle.

What was she going to say to Charley? She'd never had anyone offer to buy her a car before. Not even her own husband.

Chapter Seven

The next morning came quickly. It was Saturday and Edith had stayed up late so she could finish writing Charley's card. She knew she'd be making jelly today and wouldn't have time to finish the card later. Besides, she didn't want to risk getting any drops of choke-cherry juice on it.

She'd left the card on the kitchen table and it was the first thing she saw when she turned on the light this morning. She put some water on to boil for her tea and her oatmeal. She moved the card so she could set a place mat on the table. Then, wondering if the choke-berry juice might somehow splatter as far as the table later, she carefully took the card and set it on the top of the refrigerator. Nothing would hit it up there.

In the end, she'd just written down the plain unvar-nished truth in the card. *You are the best friend I've ever had.* That didn't seem like quite enough so she added *In all my life.* She knew Charley well enough to know that he wouldn't like a list of the things he'd done for her so she added a Bible quote from Proverbs 18 instead that said, "There is a friend that sticketh closer than a brother."

Edith had a brother when she was a young girl, but he'd died in an accident when he was ten. She hadn't thought of him for years, but recently she'd decided he would be a lot like Charley.

Edith had set aside a loaf of bread for Charley, too, and she planned to give him one of the first jars of jelly she made today. She wished she had something else to go with the card, like maybe a pound of some special coffee beans. Maybe Doris June could ask Curt if Charley had any coffee beans that he particularly liked. Charley had gotten an electric bean grinder for Christmas last year and he liked to use it. He'd told her it made him feel like he was on the edge of new technology.

After she had eaten breakfast and said her morning prayers, Edith got ready to make jelly. She had already put on her oldest housedress, a faded pink gingham one with a small tear in the sleeve. She wasn't wearing as many housedresses as she used to since Doris June had updated her wardrobe, but jelly-making was not a time to make a fashion statement.

To keep her hair in place, she tied one of Harold's old red bandanas around her head. Then she put on her oldest pair of orthopedic shoes because she would be on her feet most of the day and she didn't want to get any stains on her regular shoes.

Edith checked the small mirror in her hallway and knew she was ready to cook. She looked awful, of course, but that was how a wise woman looked when she was getting ready to make jelly. Fortunately, no one except Doris June would see her this way.

The clock on the wall said it was almost eight. Edith expected her daughter to arrive soon. The thought of the two of them making jelly together again had Edith humming as she put her breakfast dishes in the sink and bent down to take her canning pots out of the cupboard. The chokecherries were laid out on cookie sheets, ready to be crushed into juice.

She'd tried one of the small berries earlier and it was more tart than usual. Charley was right that the ones that grew near the Morgan place weren't as sweet as their usual chokecherries. But she'd just add a dash more sugar and the jelly would be as good as usual. As she admired the berries all spread out on her counters, she was happy God had given them choke-cherries instead of peaches around Dry Creek.

Doris June came and they started crushing the berries in a big bowl with forks. They had some cheesecloth ready so they could drain the berries—pulp and juice both—through the cloth and into another big bowl. Over the years, Edith had perfected a technique using a wooden clothes pin to clip the cheesecloth together so they could hang the bundle of berries and get every possible drop of juice.

It was about nine o'clock when they heard a knock at the front door.

"Oh, dear," Edith said as she looked around at the splotches of berry juice on her counter. "That's probably Charley."

"I can get it, if you don't want him to see you looking like that," Doris June offered.

"He's seen me looking worse," Edith said, although she couldn't seem to make herself go to the door. She had an urge to check her hair in the mirror instead.

"Still," Doris June said as she put down her fork, "I can get it anyway."

"Tell him to come back in an hour or so. We'll be done with the crushing at least."

Doris June was at the doorway to the dining room by then, but she looked back. "Since when do you and Charley make appointments with each other?"

"It's not an appointment," Edith said, but Doris June had already stepped out of the kitchen and into the living room. Edith wasn't sure what it was, but it wasn't what her daughter was implying.

Or was it? She tried to be honest with herself. Maybe things were just a little different between her and Charley these days. It was probably because she had a greater appreciation for him. And she felt closer to him now that she'd finally told him the secret of her early married days.

Still, it was nothing for others to worry about. If she wanted to look her best around Charley, it was perfectly natural.

"It was Conrad Nelson," Doris June announced as she came back into the kitchen and laid a business card on the table. "He said to tell you that Elmer came through with the pickup this morning so he's going back to Miles City. He wants you to call him if you have any questions about a new car." Doris June paused. "I didn't know you were buying a new car."

"I'm not. My car is good enough."

"It's beginning to burn oil though. That's never a

good sign. You could spend a lot more fixing up that old car than buying a newer one."

"I suppose. But everything isn't always about money."

Edith didn't know when it had become so complicated to own a car. It was discouraging.

Doris June walked over and put an arm around her mother. "It's okay. Maybe I can help you pay for some of the repairs your car needs."

"I think I can pay for the repairs," Edith said. "I just need to find someone to make them. The men around this town seem to have forgotten all they ever knew about working on old cars."

"Well, we'll figure it out somehow," Doris June said as she gave her mother's shoulder a final squeeze. "In the meantime, I can drive you to Miles City. I called yesterday and made us both an appointment at the beauty shop for Monday afternoon."

"Good. That would be good," Edith said as finished crushing the berries. She didn't know if Jasmine Hunter was coming, but she wanted to be ready. According to the postman, the other woman wouldn't get the letter Edith had sent until today. She figured that gave her time to buy another new dress as well as get her hair cut. Edith thought for a moment. She wouldn't mind meeting Jasmine for the first time while wearing a silk suit. Yes, that's what the occasion called for. A gray silk suit and the strand of pearls she'd inherited from her mother. And some new shoes, of course.

Edith could practically see herself talking with the other woman…and then she dropped back to the present. She needed to concentrate on the jelly and the upcoming harvest dinner or she'd say something to make Doris June curious.

"I can come over and help you make the biscuits, too." Doris June was facing away from her mother as she hung the cheesecloth with the crushed berries on the hook that had been mounted on the cabinet door for that very purpose. "I don't think you should be rolling the dough out for that many biscuits, not with that touch of arthritis in your hands."

The suspended berries quickly stained the cheesecloth red and started to drip juice into the bowl beneath them.

"I'd appreciate the help," Edith said. She always liked to share a kitchen with Doris June.

"If you want, I can churn some butter this year, too. I found an old churn out in the barn at the farm. Curt's mother must have used it."

Edith nodded. That would be Sue. "She did. She used to bring me over a dish of it and I'd give her some of my jelly."

Charley's wife had always had that same contented look that Doris June wore these days. Apparently, all the Nelson men made good husbands.

The second knock at the door came a half hour after the first.

"Now this must be Charley," Doris June said as she grabbed a paper towel off the roll and started wiping her hands. "I'll go let him in."

The mirror was in the hall outside the kitchen. Edith didn't want to go check her appearance there as she might be visible to anyone coming through the living room. She had a shiny metal toaster though and she could, at least, find out if her hair was in order by looking at its surface. She ducked down so she was level with the toaster and started pushing her hair back under that old bandana she was wearing.

Edith could hear the soft sounds of voices on her porch so she straightened up.

"There's someone here to see you," Doris June said as she walked into the kitchen. She had a small frown on her face. "It's a Jasmine Hunter."

Edith felt the blood leave her face.

"I invited her to come in but she said she'd wait on the porch."

Edith nodded as her hands went back to her hair. And then to the apron she wore over her old house-dress. She didn't know whether to tug on the apron strings or the strands of hair that were still loose from her bun. She was a mess.

"She's not—" Edith started and then stopped. The woman wasn't supposed to be here—not yet, and certainly not when Doris June was here. The postman must have been wrong about how long it would take a letter to reach L.A.

"I'll go." Edith stopped caring about how she looked. She took a step toward the living room. The main thing was to talk to the woman before she said anything that Doris June could hear.

"Wait," Doris June stammered. "Before you go, you need to know she was asking for dad."

"Oh." Edith stopped. That meant she hadn't gotten the letter after all.

"It's not the census year, is it?" Doris June frowned.

Edith shook her head. She'd go ask Jasmine Hunter

to come back at another time and then she'd think about what to tell Doris June. Maybe she could say that an old friend of Harold's had come by to see him. Maybe even a distant cousin.

She couldn't do that, she realized as she was halfway through the living room. She never had believed that lying solved anything. She stood up in front of first-graders and told them that in Sunday school all the time.

By the time Edith reached her front door, the palms of her hands were damp. She opened the door inward and there, on the other side of the screen, stood a woman.

Edith squinted. This woman didn't look like any picture Edith had imagined of Harold's lover. She opened the screen door so she could see better and the woman leaning against the porch railing took a step forward.

"Jasmine?" she asked.

The woman nodded. There must be some mistake, Edith told herself. The woman was thin, but that was the only way she resembled Edith's longstanding image of what Jasmine looked like. She wore faded jeans and a black leather jacket, both of them too large for her. Her face was pale except for a line of red across her forehead that probably came from a hat or something pressing on it. The woman put a hand up and tried to fluff her obviously dyed brown hair as Edith stared at her but it stayed flat.

There was no style to the woman, but that wasn't the main thing Edith noticed.

"You're not old enough to be Jasmine Hunter," Edith finally said.

"You know about my mother then?" the woman asked quietly. She dropped her hand back to her side and looked at Edith squarely. "I wasn't sure you would."

Edith felt her breath catch. She'd never considered that Jasmine would have a daughter. Edith couldn't tell for sure how old this Jasmine was, but…

"You're not— I mean, Harold isn't—" Edith found she couldn't say the words. They would change everything. What if Harold and Jasmine had a daughter?

"You'll have to ask him," the woman replied stiffly.

Edith could only nod. She wished she *could* ask him. Suddenly, she felt the need to lean against the doorjamb.

The woman looked at Edith more closely. "What happened to you? Is that blood?"

Edith shook her head. She took a deep breath. "I'm fine. It's berry juice. I'm making jelly."

"Seriously?" Jasmine sounded surprised. "You mean you don't just buy it?"

Edith focused on the woman. It seemed to help to have something concrete to do so she made a mental list of what she saw. Jasmine wore no makeup. She didn't look away while Edith examined her, but held herself tense and ready. Ready for what, Edith didn't know, but she liked the courage it showed. Edith would guess Jasmine was around forty, but she had none of the softness that came with age. She was still as edgy as a teenager.

"I'm making the jelly because I want to make it," Edith finally said.

Jasmine scowled. "You're not broke, are you?"

Edith didn't know how to answer that. She couldn't

believe someone with Harold's genes could stand there with that deepening scowl on her face. Harold was always laughing and joking. He was the life of any party.

And then Jasmine turned and the sun shone on her face. Edith almost reached out and touched her cheek. Now, that bone structure could be from Harold. His jaw curved in just the same way.

"I'm looking for Harold Hargrove," the woman said as she straightened up a little. "Is he home?"

"I'm afraid he's not with us any longer," Edith said gently.

Jasmine blinked. "You mean he *died?*"

Edith nodded. The woman looked disappointed so she added, "I'd be happy to talk to you though if you come back in a half hour or so. You could go over to the café and have a cup of tea while you wait."

Edith reached into the side pocket of her housedress to see if she had a dollar bill. She didn't. "I'll pay, of course. Actually, instead of you coming back here, I'll just meet you there in a little while. Just keep the bill until I come."

"I don't drink much tea."

"Of course," Edith said. "Ask Linda for whatever you want. Get something to eat, too, if you're hungry."

Jasmine shrugged. "Okay."

Edith didn't want to turn away before Jasmine did. She was just standing there, thinking. Maybe she was trying to come to terms with everything.

"I'm sorry you're too late," Edith offered. "I'm sure Harold would have liked to meet you."

Jasmine laughed sharply. "I couldn't come any sooner. I was busy."

Edith nodded. "Going to school, I suppose."

The woman straightened herself as though she'd come to some decision. "Most people call it prison. But I did learn a thing or two."

With that, Jasmine Hunter turned and walked off Edith's porch. At the curb, she swung her leg over a beat-up motorcycle and pulled a helmet on.

Those last words made Edith forget about the juice stains on her clothes and the faded bandana on her head. They even made her forget, momentarily, that Doris June was waiting for her in the kitchen.

Edith just stood there and watched Jasmine try to get her motorcycle started. The thing looked as old as Edith's car. Even when Jasmine managed to get it moving, it kept sputtering, blowing out smoke all the way over to the café. Edith wondered what Charley would say when he saw what she was driving. It would be good to remind him that not everyone had a new car and that some people's transportation was even worse than hers.

Chapter Eight

Edith walked back to the kitchen. She was tempted to sit down on the sofa and not get up until she could think everything through, but she needed to send her daughter home, at least for a while, so she could talk to Jasmine privately.

"Are you okay?" Doris June asked when her mother went back inside the kitchen. "You look a little pale."

Edith nodded. "I'm fine, but I could use some rest. Would you mind if we took a break from making the jelly? I'd like to lie down for a while. Could we start back up this afternoon?"

"Oh, I can finish the jelly by myself if you want," Doris June said, giving her mother a searching look. "I hope that woman didn't upset you."

"No, I'm fine. I just need to rest a little. The berries need to hang and drain for a while anyway."

Doris June nodded, although she didn't look convinced. "Dad didn't have any old debts, did he? Somebody he borrowed twenty bucks from and forgot to pay back?"

Edith shook her head. "Not that I know of."

"Well, if it's anything—anything at all—let me know if I can help."

"I will."

"Then I'll leave you to your nap." Doris June hesitated for a moment. "I'm sure you'll tell me all about that woman later."

Edith nodded. She prayed she'd know what to say by the time Doris June got back this afternoon. She didn't want to keep anything from her daughter now that Jasmine was here, but she needed to find the words. The right words.

After Doris June left the house, Edith gave in to her earlier urge and sat on the sofa. She needed to gather herself together before she went upstairs to change her clothes. For the first time in over a decade, she wished Harold were still alive. Then this would be his problem to figure out.

She couldn't believe that poor woman had spent time in prison. She knew, of course, that a lot of women ended up in prison for one crime or another. But to have a woman who might be Harold's daughter there… Edith just shook her head. It didn't bear thinking about.

Well, first she had to find out if the woman even claimed to be Harold's daughter. Maybe she was just looking up old friends of her mother and already knew who her father was.

Not likely, though, she thought.

Twenty minutes later, Edith parked her car by the café. She normally wouldn't drive such a short distance, but for some reason she wanted the car with her. Besides, she'd worn her best pair of shoes and there were still some mud puddles around from the rain yesterday.

After she took the key out of the ignition, Edith bowed her head. *Please, Lord, help me know what to say. This woman is precious to You. Help me show her Your love. Guide me as we talk.*

Edith straightened her dress after she climbed out of the car. She'd smoothed back her hair into its usual bun when she'd changed and she was wearing her pearl necklace. She'd dabbed a little rose water behind her ears although she didn't know if Jasmine was the kind of woman who appreciated perfume.

Just before she got to the café steps, Edith turned around and went back to the car. She opened the door and pulled the locket off the rearview mirror.

The café door was propped open and Edith walked right in. There was smoke in the air and the smell of burnt food. No one was sitting at the tables out front, but she could hear voices coming from the kitchen.

Jasmine's motorcycle was outside, leaning against the rail of the porch, so Edith knew she had to be around somewhere even if she wasn't sitting in the café like Edith expected.

The smoke got heavier as Edith walked back to the kitchen and she debated about swinging the door open that separated the cooking area from the rest of the café. It smelled like burnt bread. The fact that she heard voices on the other side of the door was what made her open it.

"Anyone here?" Edith called softly.

"Yeah," Linda answered as she stood up from where

she was sitting with Jasmine at a table. "We're just trying to figure out my toaster oven. Some wire somewhere is faulty. It just scorched half a loaf of bread."

Edith stepped closer and could see that the small oven was turned on its side. Jasmine was unscrewing something from the back of it. Edith noticed that there was no trace of a scowl on Jasmine's face as she worked on the oven.

"It's probably something in the temperature gauge," Jasmine said as she finished unscrewing a panel.

"I'll have to drive into Billings to get a new gauge for the thing," Linda said.

"Naw, I can fix it," Jasmine said, lifting the panel off the back. "I'm good at fixing broken parts."

"Well, we don't need to fix it right this minute," Linda said as she walked over to her grill. "I was just about to put your hamburger on. We can wait until after you eat. Go ahead and visit with Mrs. Hargrove out front while I get your order ready. It's not every day you get to sit down and talk with an old friend."

"Oh," Edith said, almost involuntarily.

Jasmine gave her a quick look.

"Well, yes, we have been looking forward to a visit," Edith said, finding her voice. It was the best she could do. Jasmine followed her out of the kitchen and gestured to a table with a large glass of soda on it.

"I'm sitting there," she said.

Edith sat on the side of the table opposite from where the glass was.

"Makes you nervous, doesn't it?" Jasmine said, her voice low and easy, as she slid into her chair. "Makes you wonder what else I'm going to tell people."

"What do you mean?" Edith asked.

"I'm sorry to do it this way. I'd hoped to meet your husband and ask him to give me some of what's due me. I know he's dead, but I figure that doesn't mean I'm not still owed something." Jasmine paused. "Of course, I know you have no reason to give me anything unless I threaten to make it uncomfortable for you if you don't. I've been asking Linda and it seems you're a real God-fearing woman."

Edith nodded. "I'm a Christian, yes."

"I figure a godly woman like you might be willing to pay something to keep her neighbors from knowing her husband had an affair. Even if he is dead and buried, you'd be around listening to the gossip and wondering what else people were saying."

Edith blinked. "Are you trying to blackmail me?"

Jasmine shrugged. "I figure somebody owes me something for all those missed child-support payments years ago."

"I'm sure Harold didn't know anything about a baby when your mom left here. He would have been very upset at the thought of you growing up without a father."

And it was true. Harold had been a good father to Doris June. He would have done what he could have for Jasmine as well.

Jasmine shrugged. "Doesn't matter."

"Yes, it does." Edith reached into her pocket and brought out the locket Harold had given her so long ago. "There's a picture of him in here. I thought you might like to see what he looked like at least."

Edith put the locket down on the table near Jasmine. She scarcely looked at it. Edith was glad that the kitchen door opened up just then and Linda came out with a hamburger platter in her hands.

"You probably want a cup of tea, too," Linda said to Edith as she walked over to the table. "I'll bring you one right out."

Edith noticed that Jasmine grabbed her hamburger like a woman who hadn't eaten a solid meal for a while. They were silent until Linda was safely back in the kitchen.

"You don't need to blackmail me," Edith said softly. "I'll be happy to help you as much as I can."

Jasmine nodded. "Call it what you want. It's a deal. You give me money and I keep my mouth shut."

"No, I'm not paying you for your silence," Edith said. "You're welcome to show anyone your proof and tell them all you know of what happened. All I ask is that you give me time to tell my daughter first."

Jasmine stopped eating. "So then, that money you're giving me would be, what—*charity?*" The scowl was back on her face. "I don't take charity."

"Well, I can't spare all that much so it won't be like its big charity," Edith said with a gentle smile. "But I would like to help you make a better life now that you're out of prison."

"I do fine."

"I'm sure you do," Edith said. "But if we're going to be family—"

"Whooaaa," Jasmine said. She put her hamburger back on the plate and crossed her hands in front of her like a referee. "Time out. This is nothing about being a family. I'm just looking to get my due. That's all. If your husband was my father—"

"If?" Edith asked. "You mean you don't know? Didn't your mother tell you who your father was for sure?"

Two bright spots appeared on Jasmine's cheeks and she studied the hamburger sitting on her plate. "My mother narrowed it down. There were a few possibilities."

"I see."

"Well, it's not like she was the one who was already married," Jasmine said, clenching her jaw in the same way Harold always had when he was upset. "She wasn't breaking any vows."

Edith looked at the woman sitting in front of her. What did God want her to do in this situation? Jasmine might or might not be Harold's child. Edith would have to wait to determine that. But she did know that Jasmine was God's child.

"Why don't you stay in Dry Creek for a few days?" Edith said. "That will give us time to get to know each other and sort everything out."

"There's no place for me to park my bike," Jasmine said. "I mean for the night. I usually pull under a bridge. Especially in all this rain, I can't just, you know, sit in a ditch somewhere."

"You can stay with me," Edith said. "I have a comfortable room over my garage. It's all ready for someone to use. Clean sheets and a private bath and everything. I rent it out like a hotel room sometimes. You can park your motorcycle in my driveway."

Jasmine was looking at Edith skeptically. "Are you planning to deduct money for that room from what you're going to give me?"

"I hadn't planned to."

"Good," Jasmine nodded. "I'd take the cash instead if you were. But if it's free, then thanks."

"I suppose you have big plans for the cash," Edith said. Jasmine nodded.

Edith waited for the woman to tell her more about those big plans, but Jasmine put all of her attention back on her food. It was a minute or two before Jasmine lifted her head from her plate.

"I need to see an Elmer Maynard, too. My mother mentioned him to me as well."

"He lives out of town," Edith said calmly. There was no hope that the story of Harold's affair wouldn't be common knowledge by Monday. "It's a little hard to find his place. You might be better to just catch him after church tomorrow. He goes every Sunday now. You're more than welcome to come to church, too."

Jasmine let out a bark of laughter. "Take another look at me. Do I *look* like the kind of person who wants to go to church?"

"God looks on the inside of a person. He doesn't care what a person looks like on the outside. So, yes, you might be just like the kind of person who would like to go to church if you'd give yourself some time with it."

Jasmine stared hard at Edith. "You're not going to be spouting this stuff to me if I take you up on that room, are you?"

Edith grinned for the first time since she'd met the woman. "I might. Guess you'll have to take your chances."

Jasmine looked disgusted. "Now I suppose I'll need my earplugs." She looked at Edith directly. "I bought them back down the road when I started having trouble with my motorcycle."

Edith nodded. "I noticed it wasn't running right."

"I just need a place to work so I can fix it."

"Yourself? You can fix it yourself?" Edith asked.

"Of course," Jasmine said. "That's what I took in prison—mechanic courses. Most of them were by correspondence, but I learned. They always try to teach you something in prison. Figured I could use the time inside to learn something that would be useful to me when I left."

"You learned something so you could get work when you got out? Good thinking."

"I didn't learn so I could get a job." Jasmine rolled her eyes. "I plan to have my own shop."

Edith nodded. "But if you don't get a job, how will you make enough money to start your own shop?"

Jasmine just looked at her as if she were slow-witted.

"Oh," Edith said. She understood the plan now. "I don't—that is, I do have some money, but it's not enough to open a shop."

"Well, it's not like I'm collecting for the Girl Scouts here. I thought we were talking something with some zeros behind it."

Both doors to the café—the one to the kitchen and the one to the porch—opened at the same time. Linda came out with Edith's tea as Charley walked in from outside.

Linda had no problem walking to the table where the two women sat, but Charley seemed to be glued in place. He just stared at Edith and Jasmine.

Edith waved Charley over as Linda set the cup and

saucer down on the table. A tea bag sat on the side of the saucer. "Come meet Jasmine."

Edith didn't know where this conversation was going, but she did know she would feel better if Charley were sitting here by her side. She didn't really want to talk dollars and cents with Jasmine, but she figured she would be doing good to give Jasmine enough for the woman to pay her rent for a couple of months while she settled into a job.

Charley didn't say anything as he pulled a chair out from the table and sat himself down next to Edith. Linda had gone back to the kitchen. Edith put the tea bag into her cup of hot water.

"This is Jasmine Hunter," Edith said in what she hoped was a calm voice. "Her mother, also Jasmine Hunter, used to know Harold."

Charley looked startled. "Pleased to meet you."

Edith looked at Jasmine. "I told Charley about the letter. Of course, that's when I thought it was from your mother and—"

"I used some of her stationery," Jasmine admitted. "When I was going through her things, I found the stationery and the names. Of course, she'd told me about the men earlier, just in case…"

Jasmine's voice trailed off and she suddenly looked very weary.

"I'm sorry I never asked," Edith said softly. She reached over and put her fingers on one of Jasmine's hands. Edith could feel her tense up, but she didn't pull away. "What happened with your mother?"

"She died when I was—" Jasmine looked at

Charley and then back at Edith "—you know, studying to be a mechanic."

"Oh, I'm so sorry."

Jasmine nodded. "She'd been sick a long time. Cancer."

"Did she ever marry?" Charley asked. His voice was gruff, but not unkind. "I mean, I was wondering if you have any other family."

Jasmine shook her head. "Don't need them though. I'll do fine for myself once I get my shop going."

"Of course you will," Edith said and gave Jasmine's hand a squeeze. "Besides, now you have us."

"Us?" Charley said with astonishment in his voice.

"You?" Jasmine followed in the next instant. She didn't seem as much surprised as horrified.

"Well, me, at least," Edith said. "And God, of course."

"Of course," Jasmine said and her lips twisted a little. "That's going to make all of the difference."

Edith started to smile. "You have no idea, child. No idea at all."

The three of them sat in silence until Linda brought out some coffee for Charley.

"So will you be spending the night?" Charley finally asked as he lifted his cup to his lips.

Jasmine nodded.

"Of course, she's going to church with me tomorrow," Edith said. "So she has to spend the night."

"Only to meet that other guy, Elmer."

Charley nodded.

"I'll need to tell Doris June this afternoon," Edith said. She wasn't looking forward to that.

"Do you want me to be there when you tell her?" Charley offered.

"No, it's something she and I need to face together."

Jasmine's face brightened. "Doris June? That's the woman who opened the door at your house?"

Edith nodded. "She's my daughter."

"Does she have any money?" Jasmine asked.

"We can talk about that later," Edith hurried to say.

It was too late—Edith could see anger in Charley's eyes.

She reached into the pocket of her sweater and brought out three five-dollar bills, laying them on the table. She picked up the locket she'd laid down earlier as well. Maybe Jasmine would be interested in it after she knew them all better.

"I need to get back to the jelly," Edith said. "But please stay and enjoy the rest of your lunch. Feel free to have a piece of pie, too. Or an ice cream sundae. I think Linda even has some peach cobbler today."

"I haven't had pie in years."

Edith brought out another five-dollar bill and laid it on the table. "Better have two pieces then."

"Thanks," Jasmine said, looking at her closely.

Charley looked as if he were getting ready to say something so Edith slipped the locket in her pocket and put her hand on Charley's arm. "Walk me to my car." She wasn't sure that he would, so she added, "I'm not feeling as steady as usual."

She could always count on Charley. He stood up like the gentleman he was and offered her his elbow.

Edith didn't rush to the door. Once she and Charley were out of Jasmine's hearing, she knew he would have questions for her and she wasn't too sure of the answers. She realized she'd left Jasmine's letter in the apron on the back of the kitchen door. She'd had no idea when she first read the letter that she'd be having the conversation she was having with the woman who had written it.

She looked up at Charley's face. She was sure he wouldn't believe the conversation, either.

Chapter Nine

"I hope she's not trying to get money from you," Charley said.

Edith and Charley were standing next to her car. The air was moist from the rain yesterday and it was chilly. The asphalt on the empty street was dry, but it was still muddy everywhere else. The sky was gray.

"I think she's a little nervous about her future, that's all," Edith said.

Charley got a stubborn look on his face. "Well, it's not like she's just graduated from high school or anything. She must be thirty-five or forty years old. Surely she can get by the way she has been getting by without any money from you."

Edith winced. "She's been in prison."

"She *what?*"

"People do go to prison, you know, and they're not all bad people, either."

Charley took a deep breath. "Okay, so what did she do to get sent to prison?"

"Why—I—I guess I'll have to ask her when she comes over later."

"You don't even know? She could be a murderer for all you know. They don't all get life sentences anymore. And what's this about her coming over later? I hope you're not planning to be alone with her."

"Oh, she's not dangerous, she just wants some money."

"Which you don't have," Charley added. "You don't know what she'll do when she figures that out."

"I've already told her there's no point in trying to blackmail me."

"She was trying to *blackmail* you?"

Edith felt a headache starting. "It's not like that. She's just a little awkward about money, I think. She didn't look like she'd take a penny from me when she thought it would be charity. She's got pride, that's all."

Charley shook his head. "People can have pride without blackmailing anyone."

They were both silent for a moment.

"It's just—she might be Harold's daughter," Edith said finally. Her voice softened. "Why she could almost be Doris June."

And that, Edith thought, was simply the end of the discussion. Family had always been important to her. She might not have known about Jasmine until today, but that didn't make her any less a part of the Hargrove family, assuming, of course, that Harold *was* her father.

"Just promise me you won't give her any money without talking to me first," Charley said. "I suppose some small amount is due her, but—"

Edith looked at her old friend. He was worried on

her behalf. She could see it in his eyes and in the small frown on his forehead. She'd seen his dear face for decades, but lately when she looked at him she felt some new emotion was awaiting her just out of her reach somewhere. "I always talk things over with you."

Charley nodded. "Good."

Edith heard a car go by and turned around to see that it was Doris June heading to her place. She was coming back to finish making the jelly.

Edith looked up at Charley. "I should go."

Charley nodded and then bent down and kissed her on the forehead. "Just be careful."

"I'm always careful," Edith said because she couldn't think of what else to say. Charley had kissed her. For a moment, her heart had leapt with some hope she could not name. But then everything settled down. It wasn't that kind of a kiss. It was more like the kiss of one good friend to another.

Yes, that's what it was, she told herself. "You're a good friend to me."

"Maybe," Charley said with a grimace.

"Well, of course, you are," Edith said brightly as she remembered the card sitting on the top of her refrigerator. Maybe what she was feeling for Charley these days was just a heightened feeling of friendship. "If you get a chance, stop over in a few hours. That'll give me time to talk to Doris June and get Jasmine settled in."

"How are you getting Jasmine settled in?" Charley asked with a frown.

"I'm going to let her stay in the room over my garage. And don't tell me I shouldn't. You and I both know there's no other place for her to stay. And it's cold and raining. I would do that much for a stranger."

Charley nodded. "I guess that's fine. Just remember she is a stranger. Be sure to lock the door to your house when you go to bed tonight."

"I'll be very careful," Edith said.

"Maybe when I'm over later, I'll do a quick check on all the locks on your doors," Charley said. "It couldn't hurt."

"No, it couldn't hurt," Edith replied softly as she opened the door to her car. Maybe she should wait and get Charley one of those fancy cards at the drug store in Miles City. They had cards that had music in them and pop-up scenes.

"So, I'll see you in a few hours then," Charley said as he put his hands in the pockets of his jacket.

Edith nodded and slid into the driver's seat of her car. She turned the ignition on and started backing out of her parking place before Charley started walking to his pickup.

Charley was a good man, Edith thought to herself as she drove across the street and parked in front of her house. She hoped he hadn't noticed that her feelings for him were swinging this way and that lately. She didn't know what was causing it. Maybe it was all her thoughts of Harold. But the contrast between the two men couldn't be more clear.

Doris June had the jelly syrup cooking by the time Edith went back into the kitchen. The tart smell of the berries was starting to fill the house.

"Did you get your rest?" Doris June asked when she looked up from the syrup she was stirring.

Edith nodded as she walked over to the kitchen table and pulled out a chair. "A little."

"I hope you're feeling all right. Maybe you need to see a doctor."

Edith sat down in the chair. "I've just been a little preoccupied with things."

"Oh?" Doris June turned to look at her directly.

"Maybe you should sit down, too," Edith said. *Lord, help me.*

Edith had been the one who had told her daughter that her father had died. It was odd to realize that that conversation might have been easier than the one they were about to have. There were so many ways for a beloved parent to die besides the literal one, Edith thought. Finding out her father wasn't quite the man she'd thought he was might be just as bad for Doris June.

"You remember your father…" Edith began.

Doris June looked puzzled. "Of course."

"Remember how he'd go into a room and everything would change?"

Doris June nodded.

"Your father never lacked for friends." Edith looked down at her hands. She hadn't noticed the berry stains on her fingers until now. She rubbed at them as she continued. "He liked to laugh and have a good time."

"Mom, you're sure you're all right?"

Edith looked up to meet her daughter's worried eyes. "I'm fine. Just having a little bit of a time trying to figure out how to tell you that your father did things that you don't know about."

"He didn't mortgage anything, did he?"

Edith took a deep breath. "He had an affair. The woman who was here, Jasmine, might be his daughter."

Doris June was speechless for a few seconds. Then she shook her head. "Oh, no, that can't be," she protested. "Does she have any proof? She can't just show up on the doorstep and expect us to believe that Dad had an affair."

"He did have an affair. He told me about it years ago."

"Dad?" Doris June looked bewildered. "But that's not possible. He loved you."

"He loved you," Edith said with a smile. "I wish you could have seen him holding you when you were a baby. You were the most precious thing to him. Always."

"Well, I don't believe it. There's been some mistake." Doris June stood up. "I can't believe we're even talking about it."

Edith nodded. "I can see why you'd be upset. I just wanted you to know because Jasmine might tell people who she is and—"

"She has no right to tell anyone anything," Doris June said. "For all we know, she's a complete liar."

"It might take some getting used to."

Doris June turned her back on her mother and walked over to the stove. She started stirring the syrup again. "You shouldn't believe those lies about Father, either."

Edith didn't answer Doris June. She knew her daughter needed a chance to think things through. The two women started working on the jelly again in silence.

Charley waited for three hours before he started walking over to Edith's house. He usually drove his pickup, but he wanted to spend some time in the cold air praying as he walked over. He and God had an understanding about prayer; Charley didn't have to dress anything up with fancy words for God to listen. This time though Charley felt at a loss for any words, fancy or not. This whole thing with Jasmine had him nervous. He didn't want Edith to get hurt and he didn't see how that could be avoided. *Help us, Father* was all he could think to pray.

Edith was sitting in the kitchen looking at the jars of clear red jelly that were sitting on her counter. Usually, the sight of freshly canned jelly was enough to make her feel everything was right with her world. Not now, though. Doris June had finished helping her with the jelly but she'd scarcely said a word, not even when she left.

Edith wished she'd tried harder all those years ago to find the perfect words to explain Harold's affair to herself. Maybe then she would have those words to explain it to her daughter. She knew it was hard for Doris June to accept what Harold had done. She'd grown up thinking he was infallible. He had been her rock.

Edith and Doris June had shared the mother-daughter bond, but it was Harold whom her daughter had turned to for the answers to life's problems. So of course she wouldn't take easily to the thought that he had been a mere mortal.

Not that Edith blamed her daughter for that. Harold had often seemed larger than life, especially if a person didn't know him too well.

She knew when she heard the knock on the door that

it would be Charley. Jasmine had already returned from the café and accepted the key to the room above the garage, saying she'd see Edith in the morning.

Edith stood up and walked to the door. She'd taken Charley's advice and locked it, but not because she didn't trust her guest. It was more just that she didn't feel so sure of herself in life anymore.

When she opened the door, Charley stood there in the gathering dusk.

"Come in," she invited.

Charley took off his hat as he stepped inside. He tossed it on the small bench she had for such things by the door. Then he cleaned his boots on the mat and took off his jacket, hanging it on the rack above the door.

"I'm glad to see you locked the door," Charley said as they walked over to the sofa and sat down.

Edith nodded as she reached to her right and turned on a table lamp. "It's probably not necessary, but—"

Charley nodded.

They sat there for a minute before Charley said, "Curt called."

"I suppose he told you that Doris June is upset."

Charley nodded. "Apparently, she thinks this Jasmine should have some proof of what she's saying or no one should listen to her, not even us."

Edith shrugged. "There's not much doubt that Harold had an affair with a Jasmine Hunter."

"I know. And that's really the heart of it for Doris June. She doesn't believe he would do that."

"I wonder if I should have told her back when it happened."

Charley snorted. "What was she? Two at the time?"

"Well, maybe not right when it happened, but…" Edith's voice trailed off. When would have been a good time to tell Doris June? When she was ten? When she was trying to elope with Curt? When she was grieving at her father's funeral? When she finally got married herself?

"There was no way to handle it better," Charley said. "That's what I told Curt. You're doing the best anyone could with the situation."

"Thank you." Edith told herself once again that Charley always knew the right thing to say. Which reminded her… "I have something for you."

Edith walked into the kitchen. She stopped in front of the toaster and checked her hair before walking over to the refrigerator and reaching up for the card. It had stayed well out of the way of any chokecherry juice and thankfully there were no red speckles on the card.

She straightened her dress before walking back into the living room.

"I have this for you," Edith said as she held out the card to him. "It's just part of what I'm giving you. I need to wrap up a loaf of bread for you to take home, too. And I plan to bring a plant over later."

Edith kept standing as Charley slid closer to the lamp so he could read the card. She wiped her hands on the side of her dress. How could she be nervous? It was Charley.

"I appreciate the sentiment," Charley said, looking up after he'd read the card.

"It's just that…" Edith sat back down on the sofa. "Well, you do so much for me."

Charley nodded. "Well, you mean a lot to me."

Edith didn't quite know what to say to that so she stood up again. "I bet you're hungry. And I have fresh bread and jelly that hasn't quite set."

"Sounds great."

The bread and jelly led to tomato soup and grilled cheese sandwiches.

"It's not much," Edith said as she set the soup on the table. Harold had always complained if he had soup for a meal.

But not Charley.

"There's nothing like soup on a cold night like tonight," Charley said. "Besides, you have other things to do besides cooking."

"Oh, that reminds me," Edith said, wondering how she could have forgotten. "Jasmine will—"

"—be hungry." Charley finished the sentence for her with a smile. "You go ahead and eat your soup, I'll take a couple of sandwiches out to her."

"I doubt she'll starve in the next half hour," Edith surprised herself by saying. "We can both take her something to eat a little later."

Edith realized she didn't want to pass up a chance to sit and have soup with Charley. When she first married Harold, her favorite part of the day had been when they would sit and eat together. She missed that.

Charley held his hand out to her. "Shall we pray?"

They held hands as Charley asked God to bless their food. "And we ask you to let us be patient with Jasmine as well. You know what she's been through, Father. Give us wisdom as we talk with her."

"Amen," Edith said after Charley's prayer was finished. Now this, she thought to herself as she opened her eyes, this was why having a meal together was so special.

After they had eaten, Edith made some ham sandwiches for Jasmine. She also put a couple of apples in another bag in case the woman wanted some fruit.

Charley and Edith took the food out to the garage. The clouds had lifted while they were eating and the first stars of the night had started to appear. Edith had turned the porch light on so there would be some light in the darkness as they walked. Even with the light, Charley still insisted Edith take his elbow so she wouldn't stumble as they walked across the yard.

The entrance to the room over the garage was at the top of an outside set of stairs.

"You wait down here," Charley said. "No point in both of us climbing this thing."

Edith watched Charley climb the stairs and knock at the door.

Light spilled out into the night when Jasmine opened the door. Edith watched Charley hand the bags to Jasmine. She could hear his voice, but she couldn't tell what he was saying. He appeared to be telling her more than what was in the bags, though. The woman nodded a few times and said a few words.

Before she closed her door, Jasmine waved down the stairs. Edith waved back even though she wasn't sure Jasmine could see her as she stood in the light and looked down into the darkness.

Charley made his way down the stairs slowly.

"She waved at me," Edith said happily when Charley took his last step down the stairs.

Charley grunted as he held his elbow out to Edith. "She also knows seven different ways to kill a person with her bare hands."

"What?"

"She informed me of that fact when I told her she should be sure and lock her door at night."

"Oh, well, she was just letting you know not to worry," Edith said.

"If she wanted me to not worry, she would have told me she knows how to knit."

Edith laughed a little and Charley joined in.

"Kids never tell us what will make us sleep easy," Edith said.

"I guess you're right about that," Charley said as he put his hand over Edith's on his arm. "I think we both need to remember, though, that she's not a kid."

"I know, Charley, I know," Edith said.

They were still a few feet away from the porch when Charley stopped walking. "I wonder if we can find the Big Dipper up there?"

They both looked upward and more stars had appeared across the night sky. There were still some clouds though because they couldn't find the constellation and they both knew where to look.

Finally, Edith said, "Maybe we'll see it another night."

Charley nodded. "We don't want to get chilled."

"Not when there's church tomorrow," Edith added. Neither one of them mentioned the visitor who was sure to turn heads at the service tomorrow.

When Charley left, Edith sat at her kitchen table with her Bible. Over the years, she'd done some of her best praying there. The table had changed over the years and she'd replaced her Bible a few times, too. But the knowledge that God was with her at that table never changed. She knew He cared about the heart of her family.

Chapter Ten

The morning was overcast again and Edith wondered if she'd made a mistake. She'd climbed up those outside stairs earlier this morning and knocked at Jasmine's door. The woman had called out that she'd meet her in church and Edith had taken her at her word. The church in Dry Creek was so close Jasmine couldn't miss it. No one could.

It was almost time for the church service to begin though, and there was no sign of her. Edith was standing at the top of the church steps and she could see the whole length of the street between the church and her house. It was empty. Edith decided she should have waited for Jasmine at the house.

It was cold and Edith hugged her arms to her sides. She had worn one of the new dresses Doris June had bought her and the material was too thin for a day like this. It was pink and pretty though. Edith was also wearing her pearls. Today was, after all, an occasion, she told herself. That is, it would be, if Jasmine showed up to make it one.

Charley came to stand beside her. "I couldn't find Elmer. And Curt says Doris June isn't feeling well. That's why she's not here this morning."

Edith nodded. "As upset as she was yesterday, she probably *doesn't* feel good."

"Maybe Jasmine doesn't feel—" Charley stopped mid-sentence.

Both Charley and Edith were staring down the street.

"What on earth?" Charley whispered.

Edith would have said the words herself, but she was too stunned to speak. Jasmine was walking down the street wearing a bright purple leotard, dangerously high black heels, a very short black skirt and her black leather jacket.

Odd as it was, the sight cheered Edith up immeasurably. A woman who could dress like that wasn't so set in her ways that God couldn't reach her easily enough. Edith was filled with hope.

Someone was playing the piano inside the church, but Edith barely heard the music as Jasmine walked up the steps and said, "Purple was my mother's signature color. I thought I might wear a few of her things to help remember her. I also dyed my hair brown before I left L.A. It makes me look more like her."

Edith relaxed. So that's what Jasmine's mother looked like. Suddenly the woman didn't seem so intimidating.

Edith took Jasmine's arm. "You don't need to look like your mother. You should look like yourself. I bet you have beautiful hair. What color is it naturally?"

Jasmine didn't answer. She was looking inside the church. "I haven't been to church much. But I bet you could guess that."

"Well, you look nice so don't worry about church," Edith finally said. "People here are real friendly. I'll introduce you."

"Look, I don't expect you to say who I am," Jasmine said quietly. "I don't want to embarrass you."

Edith looked in Jasmine's eyes and saw nothing but sincerity. "You can't embarrass me. It's certainly not your fault that your mother—"

Jasmine smiled slightly. "Well, it's not your fault, either. You can just pretend you don't know me."

"I most certainly will not," Edith said. "I'm pleased that you might be my daughter, of sorts."

Jasmine stared at Edith and then gave a quick laugh, shaking her head. "You're not how I thought you'd be." Edith marched into church with Jasmine on one side of her and Charley on the other. They slid into a pew near the back.

Jasmine didn't join in the singing, but she did tap her fingers against the pew in front of her during some of the hymns that had a beat to them. Edith wasn't singing so heartily herself. She kept looking around at her neighbors and friends.

She loved this place. Not that the church was so terribly unusual. There were probably thousands of little churches like this across the country all meeting about now.

She saw some plaid flannel shirts on the men and a few polyester pants suits on the women. There were good, regular people here. They would probably take Jasmine to their hearts if they knew her full story.

Jasmine shifted several times during the first prayer

and Edith could hear her leather jacket rubbing against the pew behind them. It wasn't loud, but it did announce how nervous she must be to keep fidgeting like that.

Edith patted Jasmine's knee when the prayer ended and was rewarded with a fleeting smile.

She's not just nervous, Edith realized, she's scared. *Well I would be too if I were nearly forty years old with nothing to my name, trying to make my way in a brand-new place.*

The pastor made a couple of announcements. One of them was about the harvest dinner that was coming up Friday night. Edith was glad she'd been able to make her jelly. She'd wait until Friday to make the eight batches of biscuits that she brought to the dinner with the jelly.

Once the announcements were over, the pastor asked if there were any visitors.

Edith looked at Jasmine and whispered, "Okay?"

Jasmine nodded, or at least Edith thought she did. In any event, Edith stood up.

"I have someone visiting me," she said. "Her name is Jasmine Hunter and I'm claiming her as a newfound daughter of sorts. She's here looking for the father she's never had the chance to meet."

Edith waited for the sympathetic murmur to run its course through the congregation. Then she took a deep breath and continued. "There's no need to keep secrets in all of this and you'll put two and two together soon enough anyway. It looks like her father could be Harold, my late husband."

Now, the sound wave passing through the congregation rippled with shocked gasps.

"Harold wasn't a perfect man and I'm asking you to forgive him if he's disappointed you. But Harold isn't with us now and Jasmine is, so let's all make Jasmine welcome."

Edith sat down before her knees started to shake any more than they had been.

"Well," Pastor Matthew said after a moment, "we're all children of God. We'll certainly make Jasmine welcome."

Edith didn't hear the words that followed. She felt an unexpected rush of freedom. She had told the truth about Harold and it had set her free in some way. She was finished with protecting her late husband.

She knew the people of Dry Creek well enough to know they would be kind to Jasmine. She glanced over at her. The woman had bright spots of pink on her cheeks, but she smiled at Edith.

"Thank you," Jasmine whispered.

Edith nodded and straightened her spine. She forced her hands to lie at her sides. And then she felt Charley take one of her hands in his and she relaxed. She could always count on Charley.

Charley had never been glad to have a church service come to an end, but he was this morning. He'd been proud of Edith and the warm way she'd spoken of Jasmine in front of the whole congregation, but he'd worried Edith would faint or something. He'd held her hand, her pulse was beating too fast.

Even after the final prayer, Edith and Jasmine sat still in the pew. Charley was the first one to stand, though people all around them were starting to move.

"Anyone want some coffee?" Charley asked the two women.

Edith looked at Jasmine. "They always have cookies, too."

Jasmine nodded. "I can never pass up cookies. If it's all right."

"Of course it's all right. You're a guest here," Edith said as she stood up.

Charley stepped out of the pew. People crowded around to welcome Jasmine.

"Pleased to meet you," Les Wilkerson, one of the local ranchers, said as he offered his hand. "Welcome to Dry Creek."

"If you need anything while you're here, you just let us know," Les's wife, Marla, added shyly with a handshake of her own. "I moved here not so long ago and I know it's not easy to set up a household."

"Oh, I'm not setting up here," Jasmine said in a rush. "I'm just passing through."

"Where are you headed?" asked Lance Walker, one of the hands at the Elkton Ranch.

"Oh, here and there," Jasmine answered.

"Well, I've got to say, there aren't many places better than here if you want to put down some roots."

"I'm not—I—" Jasmine stammered to a stop.

"Let's go get that coffee," Charley said as he led the two women away.

"Doesn't anybody believe in being strangers around here?" Jasmine muttered when they were halfway to the coffee table.

"Not so you'd notice," Charley said as he steered them past a group of teenagers.

"It's not natural," Jasmine muttered.

"No, I suppose not," Charley agreed, almost without thinking. He could still feel the tension in Edith through her hand as it rested in the bend of his elbow. She was a little pale, too, not that anyone else would notice.

"You really should settle someplace," Edith said to Jasmine as they reached the coffee table. "You can't just keep riding your motorcycle around the country."

"Why not?" Jasmine said, picking up a foam cup filled with coffee. She looked over the table. "I don't suppose they have—ah, here it is."

Jasmine picked up a small carton of half-and-half and poured it in her coffee.

"Maybe we should make the coffee to go," Charley suggested, looking at Edith. "They have lids you can use to keep it from spilling."

"I am a little tired," Edith admitted quietly.

Jasmine looked around at the church members as she picked up one of the plastic lids. "Fine by me."

"I put a roast in the oven to bake before I came this morning," Edith said, looking at both Charley and Jasmine. "You're both welcome to come for dinner."

"Sounds great," Jasmine said as she pushed the lid down on the top of her cup. "Let's go before anyone else tries to sell me on Dry Creek."

Charley didn't think he should eat at Edith's two days in a row. He wanted her to know that he wasn't hanging around just for the food. But, on the other hand, he wasn't sure he should leave her alone with Jasmine. He didn't quite trust her yet, though Edith clearly did. Besides, he expected Jasmine knew even more ways than seven to kill people if she had the use of a dinner fork.

* * *

Edith was making gravy to go with the roast. She'd peeled potatoes in the morning and put them on simmer so they were ready when she walked in the door from church with her two guests following her. All she'd had to do was cook some frozen corn and finish up with the gravy. She already had bread.

It was no surprise to her that Charley offered to carve the roast, but Edith had not expected Jasmine to volunteer for any tasks. She had, though, and now she was setting the table.

They were using the dining room table and the good dishes from the sideboard. The gravy could be left alone a minute or two on low heat so Edith went into the dining room to see if Jasmine needed help.

Jasmine was frowning lightly over the silverware that Edith used with her company plates. "We don't need to use these butter knives, do we?"

"Don't pay any attention to the silverware that you don't recognize," Edith said as she walked over to the open drawer where Jasmine was standing. "I don't even know what it's all for—I just use the regular knives, forks and spoons."

"They didn't give us silverware in prison," Jasmine said. "It's usually plastic, so it's kind of fun to see these weird things. Hey, is this a pickle fork? I've heard about those."

"I believe it is," Edith said, nodding at the small fork Jasmine held up. "I sent away for that silverware years ago." Edith stopped and then began again. "Probably about the year you were born. I collected box tops for it."

"That must have been a lot of box tops," Jasmine said.

"It was." Edith remembered how grand she had thought the silverware was. She figured it was the one thing she might own that was better than what Jasmine Hunter had. Not this Jasmine Hunter, of course.

"I don't suppose your mother saved box tops," Edith asked.

Jasmine shook her head. "She wasn't particularly domestic."

So Harold's lover hadn't been domestic and she'd worn purple leotards; she was nothing like the picture Edith had nursed in her mind over the years. Edith found her gravy spoon. "I'll take this and dish up the gravy. You look like you're almost done in here."

Jasmine had laid a beige cloth on the table and set three of Edith's prize china plates on it. She'd added glasses and white cotton napkins.

"Just give me two minutes," Jasmine said as she grabbed three forks from the drawer.

Edith went back to the kitchen and the gravy. "It smells good."

"Real good," Charley agreed from where he stood, stacking the sliced roast onto a platter. "How's Jasmine doing?"

"Good. She's a nice girl."

Charley grunted, but he didn't say anything to disagree.

By the time all three of them were seated at the table, Edith was ready for grace. She held a hand out to both Charley and Jasmine, and she was half surprised when Jasmine took it.

"Lord, thank You for this food," Edith prayed. "And

thank You for bringing Jasmine to us. Please help her find out all she needs to know about the man who is her father. Amen."

Edith gave Jasmine's hand a squeeze before she let it go.

The woman was sitting a little stiffly after the prayer, Edith thought. She wasn't even reaching for the bowl of mashed potatoes and Edith had deliberately set the bowl by her after she mentioned that she loved mashed potatoes.

"Are you a cult here?" Jasmine asked abruptly.

"What?" Edith and Charley said together.

"You and your church group are strange," Jasmine said. "Not that I mind if you're a cult. It's your business. I'd just like to be warned so I don't drink any funny Kool-Aid."

"We're normal," Edith said as she passed the platter of sliced beef and then added, "Well, most of us are most of the time."

"Just about like most places, I suspect," Charley added.

"Most people wouldn't be inviting me to Sunday dinner," Jasmine said. "Not when I'm asking around about my father who must have been a married man from this area, and probably was your husband."

Jasmine looked hard at Edith when she said the last bit.

Edith just passed Jasmine the mashed potatoes. "Well, maybe in that way, you're right. We're not normal."

"I knew it." Jasmine took a scoop of mashed potatoes.

Edith smiled. "You're not completely normal yourself."

Jasmine looked up and grinned. "You got that right."

The three of them ate the rest of their meal in peace. After they finished eating, Jasmine asked some questions about the roads around Dry Creek and Charley was able to answer them for her. She was worried about whether or not her motorcycle would run into problems if she decided to go out to Elmer's place tomorrow.

"Oh, I could drive you—" Edith started to offer and then remembered that tomorrow was Monday. "Unless—that is, I forgot that Doris June and I both have appointments to get our hair cut in Miles City."

"That's okay," Jasmine said. "My bike will make it. I just want to take the best roads."

"There's not much choice in what road to take," Charley said. "Only one gets you there."

Jasmine sighed. "Back in L.A. there are a million roads. At least, that's what it feels like. You always need a map."

Charley cleared his throat. "If you'd like to stay around here a while, my nephew, Conrad, has a car repair shop in Miles City. If you're interested in a job while you're here, I could ask him if—"

"Really?" Jasmine said. "If it was just a temporary thing, I might. I could use some mechanic experience before I open my shop."

Charley swallowed. "I was thinking more about something in the office. It takes quite a bit to be a mechanic."

"I studied it for four years," Jasmine said indignantly. "I've practically memorized the blueprints of every engine made."

"That's wonderful," Edith said with a smile. "You must be so proud."

"Didn't they let you work on any real engines?"

Charley asked with a frown. "I just don't see how you can learn it right without feeling the metal in your hands."

Jasmine sighed. "If I had some tools, I could show you what I can do with an engine. My motorcycle needs some serious work."

"Conrad might have some old tools he'd lend you," Charley said. "Especially if you helped him in the office with his billing. He hates to do the bookkeeping."

Jasmine smirked. "Everybody does."

"Still, it might be good experience for when you open your own shop," Edith said. She hadn't taught Sunday school for all of these years without learning to dangle the carrot in front of the horse. "It wouldn't hurt to go talk to Conrad about it."

"I suppose not."

Edith could see Jasmine was hooked. "If your bike is working you can drive it back and forth to Miles City. The garage room is yours for a few months at least. That is, if you're working."

"Thanks."

Jasmine stayed to help with the dishes and then she went back to the garage room. Edith and Charley had settled themselves at the kitchen table with a checkerboard.

"Do you really think she finds us that strange?" Edith asked Charley, midway through the game.

"I'm sure she does," Charley said as he jumped one of Edith's pieces. "Think about it. What kind of people has she known in life? Not such good ones considering she ended up in prison."

"I never did ask what she'd done to get there," Edith said.

"I did," Charley said as he moved one of his remaining pieces. "Robbery."

"Armed?"

Charley shook his head. "Not unless you count those hands of hers and the seven ways she knows to kill a person."

"I should ask her sometime what they are," Edith said with a smile. "I doubt she even knows seven."

"If she knows *one,* that's too many in my opinion."

"Well, everybody knows strangling. That's one."

"Two then, if she knows two that's too many."

Edith was silent for a moment as she made another move on the board. "I wonder what she'd look like with her hair fixed nice. And in clothes that fit."

Charley looked up from the board. "I think she'd look like Elmer."

"You think she looks like *Elmer?* Anyone can clearly see that she has Harold's jawline."

"I think she looks a little like Elmer around the eyes," Charley said. "It's hard to really tell who she looks like though now that I know her hair is dyed. I tried to figure out what color it really is by looking at her eyebrows, but I'm not sure. Maybe they're dyed, too."

"She wouldn't dye her eyebrows, would she?"

Charley shrugged. "Somebody who's been in prison would do about anything if you ask me."

They played together for a few more minutes before Edith made her decision. "We need to take her with us tomorrow to the beauty shop in Miles City. Maybe they'll know how to tell what color her hair really is. She doesn't seem to want to say."

"I don't think she'll want to visit the beauty shop—"

"If she's expecting us to guess who her father is, she needs to give us all she can to go on. If she doesn't want to go to the beauty shop, she just needs to tell us herself. It doesn't seem like she wants to do a DNA test or anything so that leaves her looks."

"But aren't you going in with Doris June? I don't think she'd want to take Jasmine along with you."

"If I know Doris June, she'll want to get to the bottom of all of this."

Charley nodded. "I suppose it would be best all around if we could figure out who Jasmine's father is. Until we solve that one, people are going to keep talking about it."

"I expect so."

Charley's words kept going around in Edith's mind for the rest of the evening. She was brushing her teeth when she realized she was glad she was going to get her hair cut tomorrow. If people were going to gossip about her—and she had no doubt that they were—at least some of the time would be spent talking about her new hairstyle instead of her marriage to Harold.

Chapter Eleven

Edith was sitting under a hair dryer at the beauty shop in Miles City. Jasmine was sitting in a chair on the other side of the place, getting some kind of a paste rubbed into her hair. The beautician said it would nourish the roots in case they had been damaged from the dye Jasmine had used.

Edith had asked Jasmine again what her real color was, in the car on the way to the beauty shop. Jasmine had surprised her by admitting it was auburn. She repeated that she'd dyed it darker in order to look like her mother—she thought the resemblance might help people remember, and in turn help her find her father.

When Edith looked over at Jasmine again, she noticed that it was the new beautician working on her hair. It seemed so long ago that Edith had worried about Charley dating her. Now she had other things to fret about. She looked to the front of the shop, to the waiting area.

Doris June was sitting there, flipping through a

magazine she could not possibly be reading since she picked it up or put it down every two minutes. Doris June had not wanted Jasmine to come, but she had, as her mother knew she would, seen the sense of trying to get more information so it would hopefully become clear if there was any basis for what the woman was saying.

Of course it hadn't been necessary to bring Jasmine to the beauty shop after all. The woman who'd cut Edith's hair said that there was no way to determine someone's real hair color underneath dye. And Jasmine had told them what they wanted to know anyway.

The notion came to Edith as she was sitting there that she might be a mother visiting the beauty salon with her two adult daughters for the first time—well, Jasmine was her stepdaughter, sort of. She wondered if there was even a word to describe a child that a woman's husband had fathered with another woman. Edith smiled a bit at the thought once again, she couldn't find a word to name the situation Harold had created.

Doris June had introduced Jasmine to the women in the beauty shop simply as a friend of the family. An old friend of the family, she'd explained, and then shrugged when someone asked how long she and Jasmine had known each other.

Edith just had to glance at the two of them to see how different they were. Doris June was built like her, tall and strong. Jasmine was thin and so short Edith wondered if she had been given vitamins regularly as a child. Doris June was almost a blonde and Jasmine said her natural hair color was auburn. Except for their jawlines, their faces didn't resemble each other much at all.

But something made Edith believe they were sisters.

Maybe it was just hope. Or maybe it was the defiant pride that she saw in each of them. Neither one of them wanted anything to do with the other. Doris June, of course, was more polished and hid her annoyance better, but that was understandable. Jasmine hadn't exactly spent her life in a finishing school.

Edith chuckled to herself as she shifted in the chair. Who knew there would be sibling problems in her family at this late date?

Of course, no one knew for sure who Jasmine belonged to, but Edith was already adopting her in her heart. The one thing Harold's affair had given her was the ability to look beyond her family for people to love.

She sighed with contentment.

A little while later, Edith looked in the mirror in front of her chair and wondered what had happened to her. Her long hair was gone and the bit that was left sort of puffed around her face. She reached up to touch her ears self-consciously. Her hair had been permed and combed and sprayed until she didn't recognize it.

"We'll need to get your ears pierced," Doris June said as she walked back to where her mother sat.

"Everything feels so light," Edith said. She had the urge to rub her hands along the back of her head to see where all of her hair had gone.

"You'll want to wear a scarf around your head this winter," the beautician said. "Sometimes when you get so much hair cut off, you really feel the cold for a while."

"It looks great," Doris June said and then leaned close to Edith to whisper, "Dad would have liked it."

Doris June had already informed her mother earlier

that her father was innocent until it was proven otherwise and so she was going to ignore the rumors Jasmine was starting.

Edith patted Doris June on the arm just as they both heard a shriek from across the room.

Someone had taken the towel off Jasmine's head.

"I look like a rat," Jasmine scowled.

Edith tried not to smile, especially because it was true. Jasmine's hair was wet and pressed flat to her scalp. It certainly didn't look full-bodied and healthy, which was what the treatment promised.

"It'll look better when it's curled," Edith said across the room. "Maybe you should get a perm."

"A perm? They're for old ladies." Jasmine turned to Edith. "No offense, of course."

Edith patted her hair.

"You just need to have them add a little body," Doris June said, crossing to Jasmine. "And maybe put in some highlights."

"I don't need highlights."

"I'm not talking anything dramatic. Just something a shade or two lighter than your color. Maybe they could even dye your hair the auburn color that you claim it is and then put in some highlights."

"I don't *claim* my hair is auburn. That's what it is."

"Do what you want with your hair. But if you're going to go around saying Dad is your father, you need to look, you know, not like a mouse. He wasn't a mouse kind of a person," Doris June said smoothly.

"Whatever you say," Jasmine muttered.

"For one thing, he didn't believe people should change the color of their hair."

"Don't tell me he stopped you from dying your hair?" Jasmine said with disbelief. "Was he strict?"

Doris June shook her head. "He was a pussycat."

Edith wished she had driven her car instead of riding with Doris June. She'd hung the locket back on the rearview mirror and she would have liked to bring it out so they could look at it. She suspected Jasmine would want to see it finally and Doris June, well, she might want to have a glance at it as well.

Edith joined Doris June at the front of the shop while they waited for Jasmine. They were both flipping through magazines when Doris June leaned over.

"I think maybe she's just mistaken," Doris June whispered to her mother. "I suppose it's possible that her mother lied to her and that she really believes what she's saying about Dad."

Edith nodded. "I'm sure she believes it."

Doris June nodded. "It just doesn't seem possible."

Edith reached over and patted her daughter's knee. She knew it was a hard thing for Doris June to accept, but she was working her way through it just as Edith knew she would.

Charley was sitting with the other men around the woodstove in the hardware store. The morning had started out gray and gotten darker until it finally hailed. Now the air was damp enough to bite through a wool shirt and the men had recently stuffed a couple of small logs into the firebox. They were discussing whether they had actually put too much wood in the fire and should be worried about chimney sparks when Elmer called.

Usually Pastor Matthew was working the sales counter and would answer the phone, but he wasn't there this morning so Les Wilkerson picked it up.

"Elmer's got a sore throat," Les called out as he hung up the phone. There were a dozen men around the stove or inspecting the merchandise on the shelves. "He said to tell everyone he won't be here today."

Charley grunted. "Since when do we need to call in? Makes us sound like a bunch of old women."

Les shrugged. He was in the middle of weighing out an order of screws. "I'm just relaying the message."

"Well, at least I know I need to get someone else for checkers," Charley said as he stood up and stretched.

"I'll play you," Burt Jones offered as he stood up as well.

Burt had lost his farm decades ago. He'd worked on the Elkton Ranch for years after that and now called himself retired. He was even worse at checkers than Elmer, but Charley wanted something to keep his mind off the conversations swirling around Dry Creek.

He set the checker table up on the far side of the store. It was well away from the stove so they wouldn't need to worry about someone walking by and accidentally tipping the board over.

Edith had told Charley that she and Doris June were taking Jasmine to the beauty shop with them today and Charley figured it was just as well. People had started talking yesterday afternoon about Edith's little speech in church and they hadn't stopped yet. Of course, he'd known people would talk. They were naturally curious and, he supposed, people needed time to adjust to what had happened decades ago almost as much as Doris June did.

He was glad Edith wouldn't be around to hear them adjusting though. Charley figured that by the time she was back in town and visiting with people, he would have been able to steer the gossip onto a more truthful path than where it was now.

"Fred says he doesn't believe it," Burt said as he scratched his head. He was studying the checkerboard even though he'd only made one move so far.

"Fred doesn't know what he's talking about," Charley said flatly.

Fred was sitting by the stove, half dozing in his chair, and he didn't appear to hear anything. It was the men, Charley thought, who were more anxious to talk about the Hargrove marriage than anyone else.

Les walked over to watch the checker game. "What people don't understand is why would Edith tell everybody her husband had been fooling around on her? That just doesn't make sense."

"It's because of that Jasmine woman," Burt answered back. "That much I get. It's just that none of us know her. Who knows if she's telling the truth? Shouldn't she take one of those DNA things? She might not even be Jasmine Hunter."

Charley moved his checker piece and said mildly, "I think we'd have to ask Jasmine why she's not demanding a DNA test. But I do know Edith seems to believe her."

Fred stirred in his chair and looked around. "Who said DNA test?"

"We're just talking," Charley said. "Don't worry about it."

It was silent for a minute.

Fred stood up and stretched. "What I really don't understand in the whole thing is how a man could cheat on Edith. I mean Edith! I'd be scared to cheat on that woman."

Charley was surprised at the floodgate of opinions that spilled out after that comment. Everyone started talking at once. The door opened and cold air blew in as the men continued to debate.

"No man likes a woman as strong as Edith."

"If you've got a nagging wife at home, I can see why you'd want a more friendly bed somewhere else, if you know what I mean."

"A woman should know how to make a man feel like a man."

"Enough!" Charley yelled.

It was only in the silence that followed that Fred looked over at the open doorway. His face went ashen.

"We didn't—" Fred started to say.

By then everyone was looking. The door had not opened up to admit a couple of more men like they had all thought. There, standing in the doorway, were Edith and Jasmine Hunter.

"We just wanted to tell you," Edith said calmly, her eyes searching out Charley's, "Jasmine got that job with Conrad. She's real excited. Thank you for putting in a good word for her."

With that, Edith turned and walked away.

Jasmine stood in the doorway and the look she gave the men in the room made them all study the floor, even though she wasn't more than a few inches above five feet tall. Her hair looked a little different after the beauty shop but her scowl was still the same.

"Men!" Jasmine made it sound like it was the lowest possible thing to be. Charley was inclined to agree with her for the moment.

"Jasmine," Edith's voice called and the other woman turned and walked away with the same dignity Edith had shown.

It took a minute or two and then the men began to speak all at once.

"We didn't—" Les said.

"I'd never—" Fred murmured.

"How could—" Burt started and stopped.

The dozen or so men in the room all looked at Charley with mute appeal in their eyes.

"Fools," he muttered as he got his hat down from the rack and pulled his jacket on. He didn't have time to talk with any of them. Not when Edith needed him.

Chapter Twelve

Edith and Jasmine were halfway back to Edith's house by the time Charley caught up with them. The ground was wet everywhere and there was still some hail on the sides of the road. He'd noticed when he stepped out of the hardware store that neither of the women was dressed for the chilly weather. He was glad to see though that Jasmine had taken Edith's arm and was helping her over the slippery ground.

"They're sorry," Charley said when he reached the two women.

Edith nodded. "It's what I always thought people would say if they knew."

Neither Edith nor Jasmine looked at him, but Charley matched his stride to theirs and kept walking with them. "They didn't mean anything by it."

"I could make them sorry," Jasmine muttered. "Real sorry."

If the woman hadn't looked like she was on the verge of tears, Charley might have been worried.

"I'm sure they'll all apologize if you let them," Charley said.

"They were only speaking their minds," Edith replied. "They don't need to apologize."

"They most certainly do." And he'd see that they did it. "If you don't want to listen to them say the words, they can very well write them down for you."

"I guess I always knew there would be talk," Edith said. They had reached the sidewalk that led up to her house. For the first time, she turned and faced Charley.

"Your hair," Charley said. He had been so upset he hadn't even noticed it until now. "It looks nice."

"I look like a dandelion," Edith said flatly.

"That's only until the perm settles in," Jasmine said. "That's what they said at the shop. Remember?"

Edith nodded. "I know what they said."

"I'm sure they never lie in those places," Charley said even though he'd never been in a beauty shop in his life. He knew the barber he went to was pretty straightforward though and he imagined people in the grooming business would all be that way.

Edith turned and started walking up toward her house. "I don't know what I was thinking. I'm a plain woman and that bun suited me."

Jasmine was walking beside Edith and there wasn't room for three to walk abreast on the sidewalk so Charley followed behind the two women.

"Your hair's real nice," he said again. "Real nice."

Jasmine opened the front door to the house and Charley noticed that no one used a key. Now wasn't the time to mention that though. Charley followed the women up the stairs and he stood in the open doorway of the house.

"I can make you some tea," Charley offered. He didn't know what to do, but he knew Edith liked her tea.

"I think I'll just rest for a bit if you don't mind," Edith said as she sat down on the sofa.

"I could stay and…" Jasmine's voice trailed off.

Edith shook her head. "I'm fine. Besides, you need to get ready to start your new job. I'll just sit here a bit."

"I can stay with you," Charley offered after Jasmine had gone to her room.

"There's no need," Edith said. "I think I'll go lie down."

"A nap would do you good," Charley said softly.

He didn't want to leave, but there was no polite way to stay. He stood there for a while though, giving Edith time to change her mind if she wanted to talk. Finally, he accepted the fact that she wanted to be alone.

"If you need me, call," Charley said as he stepped back onto the porch and closed the front door.

He'd no sooner closed the door than he opened it again. "And remember to lock this door when I shut it."

Charley figured the temperature had dropped ten degrees since he'd left the hardware store. It was a cold day in Dry Creek.

Edith was tired. She forced herself to get up and turn the lock when Charley left, but it was only because she knew he would wait out there until he heard the lock click into place. Somehow her entire life had become heavy. It was the memories—they were smothering her. All those old feelings of not being attractive enough for Harold. Of not being warm enough, or kind enough, or something enough.

And, lately, she'd been fool enough to start feeling romantic about Charley. She'd seen that right away when she'd listened to those men in the hardware store. They weren't just talking about the past; they were reminding her of the present. She wasn't a woman who gave men romantic notions. It didn't matter what decade it was, men didn't change that much.

Edith turned the lights off and walked to the stairs. It was only about four o'clock, but she needed to lie down.

She had asked herself so many times if there was something she could have done to prevent Harold's affair and she never came up with any answers. She had not had the power to make him faithful. Just like she didn't have the power to be anything other than what she was.

Edith was halfway up the stairs when it occurred to her that Harold probably told himself some of the same things those men were saying over in the hardware store. When all was said and done, he may have blamed her for the affair. Maybe that's why he'd never seemed particularly sorry for having it.

She lay down on her bed and covered up with a quilt she'd made years ago. She felt cold down to her bones.

Charley stood on a stepladder and pulled a roll of white paper off one of the top shelves in the hardware store.

"I think that's supposed to be for lining cabinets," Les said as he held the ladder steady. "It doesn't quite seem good enough for what you want."

A half-dozen men were gathered behind Les.

"Maybe we should wait and get some fancy paper from that stationery place in Miles City," Burt suggested.

"What stationery place? You mean that gas station with the birthday cards?" Les asked.

"They're not all birthday cards," Burt protested.

"We don't have time to wait," Charley said. He wanted the guilty parties to write down their apologies before they got drawn off into other business and forgot all about what they'd done. He grabbed the roll of paper in one hand. "This will do."

"I don't know," Fred said as he looked up at the paper. "Women seem to like things to be a little prettied up."

"I've got that covered," Charley said as he handed the paper down to Les. "Jasmine is going to come over and do some drawings."

After Charley had made sure Edith had locked her door, he decided he should make sure Jasmine remembered to lock hers, too. When he told her how sorry the men were for what they'd said and that he was going to have them write down their apologies, she'd offered to help in any way she could. He'd told her to come over to the hardware store in twenty minutes.

"My writing's not that big," Burt said when he looked at the roll of paper. "I don't think I can fill up the page."

"We're going to try," Charley said as he stepped down from the ladder.

The floor by the woodstove was the only area big enough to roll out the paper so the men had to lower themselves to the floor to do their writing. That alone took five minutes. Charley gave them each a thick black marker to write their most sincere apology. He was saving the colored markers for Jasmine's use. He was hoping she had some artistic ability and could make the paper look special in some way.

"I was thinking you could maybe add flowers," Charley said later when Jasmine arrived at the hardware store. The long sheet was laid out in front of them with the apologies in big block letters.

"I've never done flowers," Jasmine said with a frown. "I draw the insides of engines."

"Well, certainly you've drawn other things," Charley said hopefully. "Maybe when you were little?"

"I drew cartoon characters for a while," Jasmine said. "I was pretty good at it, too."

Charley handed all of the colored markers to Jasmine.

"Do your best," he said.

The men were now sitting around the stove in their chairs, trying to think of more apologetic things to say to fill in the white space.

"You mentioned we're idiots?" Fred asked Burt.

"Twice for me," Burt nodded. "Three times for you."

Fred turned around to look at him. "Why more for me? I didn't say anything other people weren't thinking."

"Four for you," Burt said as he stood up and walked to where Jasmine was stretched out on the floor, drawing.

"If anybody's going to call me an idiot, it should be me," Fred said.

"There's lots of room left," Charley said, holding up a marker for the man.

Fred didn't take it though. He just sat in his chair.

"I still think we should send flowers," Les said from where he was crouched over, writing in a far corner. "Marla sure likes it when I get them for her."

"This is Edith. We're not *courting* her," Burt said.

"Maybe we should be," Charley said. He was standing now, watching Jasmine as she worked.

"Seriously?" Fred sat up straighter in his chair. Then he looked down at the roll of paper where Burt was still writing. "You're not putting anything there that's romantic are you?"

"Me?' Burt looked up with a blank look on his face.

"You're idiots for sure if you don't appreciate someone like Edith," Jasmine said fiercely.

"Well, she can cook," Fred said.

"Those biscuits of hers are the best I've ever eaten," Burt nodded. "And her pies. She makes good pies."

"She deserves better than any guy here," Charley said.

The door to the hardware store opened just then. It was late afternoon and everyone looked up at the sound.

It was Elmer. At least, Charley thought it was Elmer. It was hard to tell because of the wool blanket he had wrapped around him like he was an Egyptian mummy. He had on his winter clothes under the blanket and his face—what Charley could see of it—was pinched with cold.

"Do you need a doctor?" Charley asked. "I can drive you into Miles City."

Elmer opened his mouth and a croak came out. He tried again. "No one told me."

"If you're not going to the doctor's, you should be home in bed," Charley said.

Elmer tried talking again, but no sounds came out of his mouth at all. He looked like an actor in some nightmare play. Finally, he just pointed at Jasmine.

Charley figured it out. "Jasmine Hunter. Come meet

Elmer Maynard. I'd recommend not shaking hands yet though."

Jasmine stood up and looked Elmer over. Charley figured no one would want to claim a feverish man in a blanket as kin so he didn't blame her for just looking.

"The two of you can talk later," Charley said. So far, the people in Dry Creek didn't know that Elmer could also be Jasmine's father and Charley thought it best to keep it that way for today.

Jasmine nodded as she turned back to the section of paper she was working on.

"Call when you feel better and I'll bring Jasmine out to see you," Charley offered with a nod to Elmer.

Charley didn't know why he was getting so involved. He hoped he wasn't going to feel as protective of Jasmine as he did Edith and Doris June. The woman had been able to make it up here from Los Angeles, she should be able to make it down the road to Elmer's place.

The other man nodded at that, but he kept looking at Jasmine for a bit anyway. Then he turned and left. The men watched him go with puzzled expressions but before they could say anything Les let out a whoop from where he stood at the counter and announced something about a deformed nail he'd found in the bin he'd been sorting. It apparently looked like the tail of Boots, a dog they all knew. The men of Dry Creek never could resist a wonder like that and they all went over to take a look and give their opinion.

Except for Charley. He'd seen enough wonders for the day. So he went and sat down on the floor next to Jasmine.

"It's not him," she said softly.

Charley looked around to be sure no one was close enough to hear. He knew she was talking about Elmer. "Oh?"

Jasmine nodded as she colored in the dress of a cartoon figure she'd drawn on the paper. Then she whispered, "I think it was Harold."

Charley couldn't help but notice that the cartoon figures the woman had been drawing all looked a little like Edith.

"Edith is still going to let you stay over the garage for a while, regardless of who your father is," Charley said, keeping his voice down.

"But it wouldn't be the same, would it?"

He resisted the urge to pat the woman on her shoulder. He didn't think she'd welcome it. So he settled for the next best thing. "Nice drawings."

"Thanks."

Charley continued to sit with Jasmine, watching her add some hearts and flowers to the roll of paper the men had written on. The longer he sat there, the more he realized he had something in common with this woman. They both wanted to be part of Edith's family and neither one of them had the courage to just come out and say so.

And the worst of it Charley told himself, was that he was old enough to be Jasmine's father. She might have time to wait, but he didn't have that many years ahead of him to gather up his courage. If he wasn't going to say something to Edith soon, when was he planning to do it?

Of course, today wouldn't be good. Edith was

talking a nap and it didn't seem right to wake her up to plead his case. But if he waited until tomorrow, that day could have its own problems. It seemed every day lately had something to worry over. It was foolish to think there would ever come a day perfect enough for a proposal such as his.

Chapter Thirteen

Edith was cozy under her quilt. She'd fallen asleep while she was praying last night and she woke up this morning to remember how much God loved her. She'd forgotten the feelings of flatness that came with the depression she'd had after Harold's affair until the men in the hardware store reminded her. She used to actually think those things about herself. She had felt so hopeless, like she was the eternal ugly duckling floating in a lake of ever-changing beautiful swans.

God had settled those feelings in her years ago though, and His love came flooding in this morning as the sun shone through the frost on her upstairs window. God loved her—Edith Miller Hargrove, wife of Harold Hargrove, mother of Doris June Hargrove and precious daughter of the King. She was a beautiful swan.

It might be cold outside for the moment, but the day would grow warmer. Edith lifted the quilt and swung her legs over the side of her bed. She'd wear her mother's pearls today. She always felt dressed up when she had those pearls around her neck.

Edith opened a new jar of chokecherry jelly to spread on her toast for breakfast. And then she sprinkled some golden raisins and brown sugar on her oatmeal. She was having a feast. When she finished eating, she brought her Bible in from the living room and read a few of the rejoicing Psalms.

After Edith finished praying, she stood up and walked to the front door to welcome the day. The cool air came through her screen door and she took a deep breath.

Then she looked down and saw a black garbage sack lying on her porch in front of the door. She was glad that she'd had such a reassuring time with God this morning or she might be annoyed that someone had left a sack of garbage at her door.

Not that it looked like there was much garbage in the bag. The night frost had left a thin film of white on the dark plastic. She looked closer and saw a piece of paper taped to the side of the bag. The words were smeared from the night's moisture, but she could see that they read Look Inside.

Edith opened the screen door enough to slip outside. She touched the bag and heard the rustle of paper before pulling it into her house. She set the bag on the rug inside her front door as she bent down to untie the knot that held it closed.

What was this? She pulled out a long stretch of paper that had been rolled into a tube and tied with a piece of twine. She went to get her scissors to cut the twine so she could see what the paper said. She could see enough marks to know that on the other side of the paper there were words.

By then, she suspected what the roll of paper contained and, when she had it laid out flat so she could read it, she smiled to herself. She was right; it was an apology scroll. Even with the protection of the plastic bag, the writing had been smudged a little. She could still clearly make out the words of the men though—Burt with his misspelled confessions and Les with his small, cramped printing. And, there, to the side, she saw something Fred must have written.

She knew these men were sometimes nervous around strong women. The fact that Burt and Fred had never married spoke to that. Even Les had taken his own time to find a bride. But she had to say they had put their hearts into this apology.

The drawings lining the sides of the paper confused her until she realized Jasmine must have done them. They did not look like a man's drawings. Some of the figures Jasmine had drawn were quite graceful, as if she'd had a ballet performance going on in her head at the time.

Edith left the paper stretched along her living room floor while she went back to the kitchen to make herself a cup of tea. She supposed she should write a note to the men thanking them for their words, just to let them know that she had no hard feelings.

She knew Charley was the one who had engineered the apologies, of course. He was always her defender. Still, the men had obviously thrown themselves into the task and she was touched. She didn't think any of those men even sent Christmas cards so it must have taken some effort for them to think of as many ways to say they were sorry as they had. They weren't accustomed to the social niceties.

Which reminded her. She needed to get a plant ready to take over to Charley for his housewarming gift. She had forgotten to buy a plant when she was in Miles City yesterday so she would just pick the best of the houseplants that she had. That might be better anyway because she would at least know that the plant was healthy.

Edith picked out a nice jade plant in a terra-cotta pot and wrapped shiny silver foil around it that was left over from last Christmas. She found a lavender ribbon to go with it, because she wanted Charley to know she was giving him a housewarming gift and not an early Christmas present.

She was almost ready to put her jacket on and take the plant over to Charley when Doris June called.

"How's the hair?" Doris June asked after she'd said hello.

Edith put a hand up to touch her head. "I haven't even checked this morning. Let me go look in a mirror."

"No need. I'm going to come into Dry Creek in a bit and I have some gel that might calm it down a bit. Just give me a few minutes to get there and we'll figure it out."

"I'd appreciate that," Edith said.

After that, she went over to the small mirror in the hall and looked at herself. She grimaced; she was still a dandelion head. Or she would be if her hair had been completely white instead of just graying.

Even Doris June shook her head a little when she

came to the door ten minutes later with a tube of something in her hand.

"I didn't know you used gel on your hair," Edith said as she followed Doris June into the kitchen.

"I don't. This is Brad's."

Edith frowned. "I'm not sure a teenage boy's hair product is what we need."

"Maybe not," Doris June agreed, "but it's what we have. I promised him we wouldn't use it all so stop me if I get too generous."

"I can do that," Edith said as she sat down in one of the chairs by the kitchen table. Doris June took an old dish towel out of the drawer and shook it before putting it around Edith's shoulders.

"Are you sure we need a towel? This isn't going to change my hair color or anything is it?"

Doris June didn't seem to hear. Unfortunately, Edith was now facing the kitchen wall instead of Doris June so she couldn't even see what color the gel was. She could smell the stuff though. It was a woodsy smell that reminded her of wet tree bark.

"You know, I've been thinking," Doris June said as she ran her hands over her mother's hair. "If Dad did have that thing with Jasmine's mom, I think he must have been sorry."

"I suppose he was." Edith didn't offer more than that. She knew her daughter needed to figure this out on her own.

"I mean he got you that locket. The one you keep in the car."

Edith smiled. "He gave me that locket when we got married. It has our wedding pictures in it."

The cool gel seeped from Edith's hair down to her scalp.

"But he was a good man."

"Good men can make mistakes," Edith said gently. "It doesn't mean you can't still love them."

Doris June rubbed the back of her mother's head. "This stuff is supposed to foam up a little."

"I'm sure it'll work fine."

"You don't suppose—" Doris June began and then stopped for a second before continuing. "You don't suppose Curt would ever cheat on me?"

"No, I don't," Edith said firmly. "Those Nelson men are a breed apart. I swear they'd be faithful no matter what."

"That's what I thought," Doris June said.

Edith wondered if she shouldn't get a bigger plant for Charley. Maybe even a bush for his front yard. Of course, he was only renting the Jergensons' house. He probably couldn't plant a bush in the ground and a bush would never survive the winter if it was in a large pot on the patio.

Still, the man deserved some recognition for the values he held dear. Edith was fortunate to have a man like him for a friend and she knew it. She wouldn't want to do anything to upset that friendship, which meant, of course, that she needed to ignore the fluttering feelings that had started to plague her whenever Charley was around.

It was afternoon before Edith was ready to walk over to Charley's place. She'd given the gel plenty of time to dry so she no longer looked like a dandelion. She looked more like an old-fashioned mop. Her hair undulated—wave after wave of crimped hair covered her head. It really didn't look so bad though.

Even Jasmine had said she liked the hairstyle when Edith invited her over to share lunch. Since Jasmine wasn't starting her new job until next Monday, Edith suggested she take some time to get to know Dry Creek better.

Jasmine seemed to think that was amusing, saying she'd already seen the one horse in town, but Edith just smiled and told her to go visit the big red barn that stood on the outskirts. That place had history, Edith told her. It had been built a hundred years ago. Jasmine at least seemed impressed by that. She was more interested in the graveyard behind the church though.

"That's where the good stuff is," Jasmine said as she stood in the living room with her jacket on. "People always tell their secrets on their tombstones."

"Really?" Edith had not noticed that.

"Well, not intentionally," Jasmine admitted as she walked to the door and opened it. "But you can tell by looking at the dates on things."

After Jasmine left, Edith smoothed down her dress. She was wearing a sky-blue print with large white flowers on it. It was one of the dresses Doris June had bought for her and it looked so nice with the pearls. Then she went to the mirror in the hallway. When they were at the beauty shop yesterday, Doris June had bought her a new tube of lipstick to go with her new hairstyle and Edith wanted to put a little on before she went over to Charley's.

After she put the lipstick on to her satisfaction, she smiled at herself in the mirror. Think beautiful swan, she told herself. Confidence was a woman's greatest beauty aid.

Edith didn't want to ruin the look of her dress with her regular jacket so she reached for the navy shawl she kept on the coatrack by the door. Then she was ready to go to Charley's.

Charley had just straightened his tie for the tenth time. He was tempted to yank the thing off, but he'd decided to dress like a man who was serious and, to him, that meant white shirt, suit jacket and tie. He did make a note to buy another tie though. He couldn't remember the last time he'd worn this one and he didn't care if he never wore it again.

Finally, he couldn't stand it any longer so he picked up the rose bouquet that he'd bought in Miles City this morning, opened the door to his house and stepped outside. He had debated about buying a box of chocolates to go with the flowers, but he couldn't decide what kind of chocolates to get so he finally decided to rely solely on the flowers.

It was a courageous move, and not the only one he was going to make today.

Today, he was going to propose. He was going to stop being a coward. He was going to put it all out there on the table and see what happened.

Oh, so much could happen.

Charley stepped back into his house and closed the door. He didn't know if he could face Edith day after day if she refused his proposal. And face her he would have to. There was no avoiding someone in Dry Creek. The town was much too small for that.

Well, he would just move to Miles City if she said no, Charley told himself as he opened the door again. Conrad could use some help with that garage of his. Charley forced himself to step through the door again. It wouldn't be so bad to live in exile. Napoleon had done it. Charley closed the door behind him and turned to the street. He was committed to continuing until he remembered that Napoleon had died in exile. Hadn't he? Alone and before his time?

Charley comforted himself with the knowledge that Napoleon hadn't faced any Montana winters. If he'd been a rancher from this area, Napoleon would have survived his Waterloo and never would have been exiled.

Charley put one foot in front of the other and was well on his way down the road to Edith's house when he saw a mirage. Edith was walking toward him. It was like one of those advertisements on television where the man and the woman see each other across the field and go running into each other's arms.

Of course, there was no field here. The asphalt road was wet and hard. There was no running, either. Edith looked as if she had slowed down her walk since she saw him coming. As for falling into each other's arms, well, he didn't even want to know the odds on that one. He had to have some hope to just keep on walking.

Charley had prepared his speech in front of the mirror this morning, but when he got to Edith all he could think of to say was, "Hello."

"Nice morning," she said back to him.

Charley had expected to be in Edith's living room and he'd practiced his words with that in mind. He was going to ask how her furnace was doing now that the weather had turned colder. It seemed a funny thing to say standing in the middle of the street like this, though.

"I have some roses for you," Charley said as he held the bouquet out to her.

Unfortunately, she had a potted plant in her hands so he was left holding the bouquet out when there was no way she could accept them.

Charley pulled his arm back. "I'll just hold them for you."

"Thank you. They're lovely," she said.

"Not as lovely as you."

"That's so kind."

Charley took a deep breath and made his dive. "It's not kind. I want to marry you," Charley said, all in a rush so he could breathe again.

"Marry me? *Marry me?*"

Charley didn't like the shocked look he saw on Edith's face. He'd forgotten there were no chairs to sit on when they were standing in the middle of the road like this.

"Well, yes," Charley managed to reply.

Edith just kept looking at him. "Why?"

Charley hadn't expected any questions, least of all that one. "Well, we're already good friends and our children are married so we're halfway to being family already and, well, it just seems right." He couldn't say the words he wanted to say—they stuck in his throat.

"Oh," Edith said, as if she were disappointed. But she must not have been because the next thing Charley knew she was holding out a plant. "I brought you this. For a housewarming gift."

"I know it's unexpected," Charley said. "But I just had to—"

"I know," Edith said curtly. "I should have known you would do something like this. And it's so gallant. But there's no need. I've completely forgiven the men yesterday and their talk. I mean to stop there on my way home and tell them that all is well. I don't feel bad at all anymore."

"You think I proposed to make you feel better?"

"Well, of course," Edith said. "I can always count on you to come to my rescue. And, really, I appreciate it. You must have been up all night thinking of what you could do to make up for what your friends said."

"No one proposes to make a woman feel better," Charley protested. Edith wasn't even looking at him.

"That's why you're so special," Edith said, staring down at the plant. "This was supposed to be a house-warming plant, but I think I'll give it to you as a friendship gift because you're really such a good friend."

Charley didn't see what he could do except to take the plant. He managed to give her the roses before she turned around to walk back down the street. Charley just stood and stared as Edith climbed the steps up to the porch of the hardware store.

He took back everything he'd ever said about Napoleon. Charley wasn't so sure he would have survived a Waterloo, either, not if it had anything to do with understanding a woman, which it probably did. Even a man like Napoleon must have been undone by his Josephine.

Chapter Fourteen

Edith knocked on the edge of the door to the hardware store before she walked into the room just so the men would all know she was there. She didn't want to sneak up on them again. At least not while the topic of her marriage was on their minds.

She wasn't feeling quite herself since her talk with Charley, but she had planned to speak to these men and she didn't see why a proposal should deter her. No good ever came from putting off unpleasant tasks.

If Charley had given any hint that he might grow to love her, she would have accepted his proposal on faith that love would come. But she'd already had one empty marriage; she didn't want another. Especially not with Charley, who she was almost ready to admit she no longer thought of as just a friend.

Therefore, the best thing she could do at the moment was talk to the men right here and make sure the gossip died as quickly as possible so that Charley could forget he'd ever made such an offer.

Burt was the first one to look up at her. He was playing a game of checkers with Fred. The two men were seated at a small table beside the potbelly stove and they each had their legs stretched toward it for warmth.

Edith knew Burt saw her because his face flushed red and he looked down again at the checkerboard a little too quickly.

She set her rose bouquet on the counter so she could take off her shawl. She wanted to properly acknowledge the apology the men had given and that meant she had to look like she was doing it intentionally.

None of the men were looking at her directly so Edith finally cleared her throat. That made them look up. Of course, it also made them start to talk.

"We're sorry—" Fred said.

"We never—" Burt mumbled at the same time.

"I didn't—" Les said from behind the counter.

Edith held up her hand for silence. "I know you're all sorry. I wanted to say that your apologies were very nicely done. I assure you there are no hard feelings on my part."

There was a minute of silence while the men looked at each other. Then their voices erupted again.

"We can never—" Fred said.

"So kind—" Burt mumbled.

"The best—" Les said.

"We all make mistakes," Edith said in her Sunday school voice. "What's important is that we forgive each other and move on."

Ordinarily, Edith would have said her piece and gone back home. But Burt had asked if she wouldn't like to sit a while and warm herself before she went back out in the cold and it sounded wise to do so. She wanted the men to know she was at ease with them and anything they had to say about her past marriage. By the time Edith had gotten warm, Fred was pleading with her to play him a game of checkers since Burt wasn't interested in losing another match.

Edith didn't want to refuse such a friendly offer and soon she was committed to playing Burt a game as well. By the time Les brought her over a cup of tea, served in their best visitor mug, a good hour had passed and no one had even glanced up to see Charley looking in the window as he walked by not once, but twice.

Charley was packing. He had to move to Miles City. Not only had Edith broken his heart, she'd also stolen his friends. He might as well spend his days worrying about flat tires and those pinging noises in cars. At least at Conrad's garage he wouldn't constantly be reminded of what his life might have been like.

Of course, he realized he couldn't leave without getting his mug back from the hardware store. Years ago, each man had brought his own mug for the shelf by the coffeemaker and Charley had made the mistake of bringing his favorite one. His grandson, Brad, had given him that mug for Christmas one year. It said World's Greatest Grandpa. Well, Charley knew he couldn't leave that mug to Burt. Or Fred, either. Or even the pastor. The bond between a man and his grandson was sacred.

Charley waited for Edith to leave the hardware store. And he was none too happy with how long she spent there. Most women would at least go home, have a cup of tea, and think a bit about the proposal they'd just turned down.

But not Edith. Charley had never realized the woman liked to socialize as much as she did. She was in there laughing with the guys as if she hadn't just refused someone's hand in marriage only minutes earlier.

Well, Charley admitted, she hadn't so much refused his proposal as not believed he was serious when he made it. He didn't know what was worse. One thing he did know was that he was giving up on being friends with women. Edith could just find another good friend—he was going to Miles City and Dry Creek wouldn't see him anytime soon.

It was four o'clock before Edith left the hardware store and went home. Charley put his hat on his head and set out to get his mug.

"Hey, you should have been here," Les said from behind the counter when Charley walked into the store. "Did you know Edith was a good checker player?"

"Not surprised." Charley hadn't known that, but she was good at everything else she did so it made sense. Charley started toward the coffeepot.

"Beat me ten times," Burt said, his voice filled with contentment. "A real lady about it, too."

Charley picked his grandfather mug up from the shelf.

Fred chuckled. "That ain't the only way she's a lady."

Charley put his mug down and turned. "What's that supposed to mean?"

Fred smiled. "Just that she's looking pretty good. New haircut. Lipstick. You know what that means."

Charley stepped away from the counter. "No, what does that mean?"

Fred put his hand up. "Don't get so riled. All I'm saying is that she's giving all the signs of a woman who's looking for a man."

"Well, if she is, she's not looking around here."

Fred smiled again. "I'm thinking she might be interested if she were courted properly. You know, flowers, candlelight dinners, that kind of thing. Even a classy woman like Edith would weaken if a man went about it right."

"I thought you were just saying she nagged Harold into—" Burt stopped. "Well, you know."

"A man can change his mind," Fred said.

Charley didn't say anything, but he knew in that moment he couldn't leave Dry Creek. Not yet. Not if Fred was going to pester Edith into having some kind of a courtship with him. It was one thing to leave her in relative peace. But he wasn't leaving her to Fred.

It was almost dark when Charley left the hardware store. He had stayed around to hear Fred's plan to woo Edith. Not that it showed any imagination. So far, it seemed like his big idea was to invite Edith to have dinner with him at the café.

Charley figured Fred didn't have a chance. He had eaten dozens of meals with Edith at the café and she had never thought of one of them as a date. And that was the problem, Charley realized. Fred had never taken Edith to dinner before. So, when he did invite her, she would know it wasn't just a friendly invitation.

I've just been too good to the woman. No wonder she doesn't believe I'm serious about her.

Charley was halfway home when he saw Jasmine ride back into town on her motorcycle. She really needed to get that thing looked at. It sounded like a bucket of bolts was just rattling around inside that bike. And, here it was, almost dark, and she didn't even have her headlight on.

When Jasmine stopped to say hi, Charley invited her to dinner with him at the café. She was looking a little less starved since she'd been living over Edith's garage, but she could use another hot meal.

Once Charley and Jasmine were seated at a table, Linda came over with her order pad. "Meat loaf's the special tonight with baked potatoes and a vegetable medley."

"Sounds good," Jasmine said.

Charley agreed.

Jasmine had eaten half of her food when she looked up at Charley in alarm. "I forgot. I should call Edith. She'll worry about me since it's after dark. She knows the headlight on my bike has been flickering."

"Well, you shouldn't be driving it without a headlight. I noticed it wasn't on."

"It's okay in the daytime. I try not to drive it after dark."

Jasmine asked Linda's permission to use the café phone to call Edith. When she came back, she looked puzzled though.

Charley felt the sudden worry clutch at him. "Is something wrong with Edith?"

Jasmine shook her head. "She just sounded surprised that you'd invited me to dinner." She paused and then looked him squarely in the eye. "You're not my father, are you?"

"Me? No, I never—I never even met your mother."

"Oh," Jasmine said, sounding disappointed. "If it couldn't be Harold, I wouldn't have minded it being you."

Charley decided they should both have some pie for dessert. Maybe tonight they should even go à la mode. It wasn't every day that someone wanted him for a father.

Edith set the phone down and went back to her kitchen table. A cup of herbal tea sat there, waiting for her to drink it. Her mind kept going over the conversation she'd had with Charley today and she'd gotten so lost in thought several times that she'd forgotten about the tea completely. Now, it was cold.

She held the cup anyway. She knew Charley hadn't been serious, of course, but she had pictured him home about now doing what she was doing, which was to think of what might have been if he had been serious about them getting married. Instead, he was out having a good time at the café.

And he was obviously not so broken-hearted by her refusal that he couldn't ask another woman out to dinner. Jasmine was younger than Charley, but lots of men wanted to date younger women.

Edith told herself it was just as well she was fighting off the images of living with Charley that had taken hold of her mind. Not that she could block them out completely. She could still imagine waking up in the morning to the sight of his dear face. And having him across the table from her on nights like tonight when she had to admit it was a little lonely in her house. Or sitting beside him in church knowing God had blessed her with such a man.

There were so many kinds of love, even within one relationship—she'd learned that with Harold. Her feelings for him could shoot up in triumph one minute and then crash to the bottom the next. She never felt confident in Harold's love. Even before the affair, she'd never felt secure with him.

But her love for Charley was completely different. She had loved Charley as a friend for what seemed like her whole life, and she trusted him more than any man she'd ever known. And now, she admitted, she loved him in an entirely new way. The happy flutter of romantic love she'd felt for him was not like the quick, desperate love she'd felt for Harold in the early years. It was steady and strong, like Charley himself. The man's whole character was like bedrock.

She thought of the look on his face when she'd turned him down and wondered if he could have meant something more by his proposal. Maybe some of the feelings that were awakening in her were also stirring in him.

Edith chided herself for being so silly. Of course he hadn't meant anything by it. If he had, he wouldn't be out with another woman right now. She stood up and went to turn her teakettle back on. She wasn't going to bed anytime soon, not with these thoughts swirling around in her mind.

Chapter Fifteen

The ringing of the phone woke Edith at nine the next morning. She was usually awake by seven. It took her longer than usual to realize what was happening and to pick up the phone beside her bed.

"You okay?" Doris June asked.

"Fine," Edith mumbled as she propped herself up against her pillows.

"I just thought you'd like to know you have a *boyfriend*." Doris June literally sang the word.

Edith's heart leapt. Maybe Charley *had* been serious. The first people he would tell if he was really thinking about getting married again would be Curt and Brad.

"What do you mean?" Edith asked breathlessly.

"Someone was already by the farm this morning asking what kind of flowers you like."

"Oh." That didn't sound like Charley. He had already given her a beautiful bouquet of roses. "Who?"

"Fred Wagner."

"Fred Wagner?"

"Don't act so surprised. That man would be lucky to have you as a date."

"But Fred doesn't—why, he doesn't even go to church unless it's Christmas," Edith protested. There were rumors that he called himself a closet Christian, but that didn't impress her. She wasn't even sure there was such a thing.

"I hear he's thinking of asking you to go to the harvest dinner with him." Doris was still acting like this was good news. "That counts as church."

"But I have my biscuits."

"Your biscuits aren't your life."

"Well, no, but it's not easy to get them to the church basement while they're hot. And then I have to set them up in their baskets. And put the jelly out. A man would just be in the way."

Doris June was quiet for so long that Edith wondered if they'd lost their connection.

"It's Dad, isn't it?" she finally said quietly. "He's ruined you for other men."

"No, he hasn't. But that doesn't mean I have to go out with Fred Wagner to prove it."

"Well, it couldn't hurt. You always used to tell me that a date was just a date and I didn't have to marry the guy."

"That was when you were sixteen. And I regret letting you date at all that year. I should have made you wait until you graduated from college."

"Still, the same principles apply. It wouldn't hurt you to get out a bit in that way."

"But I'm already going to the harvest dinner."

That argument didn't sway Doris June and finally Edith agreed to consider Fred's request to accompany her if he asked. She knew Fred well enough to know that he'd probably forget the idea completely before he even saw her next.

Charley wished Fred would forget his plan. Or at least find someone else to bore with the details.

Charley had made the mistake of stopping by the hardware store on his way into Miles City this morning. He had gotten the make and model of Jasmine's motorcycle and he was going in to pick up a new headlight for her. Fred, unfortunately, had wanted to ride along and Charley had agreed to take him before he knew Fred was going in to buy some flowers for Edith.

"You know the woman," Fred was saying. The two men were in the cab of Charley's pickup about ten miles outside of Dry Creek. "Don't you think she'd like some carnations more than these Gerber daisies Doris June was talking about?"

"I doubt you can get Gerber daisies this time of year."

"I don't even know what Gerber daisies are. Maybe she'd like just the regular ones."

"I bought her roses," Charley said.

"Roses! That'd sure set a man back. It's only a first date."

"Well, and she hasn't said yes yet," Charley added. He'd already heard the grand plan and he knew Fred wasn't scheduled to ask Edith to go with him to the harvest dinner until he returned with the flowers. As far as Charley was concerned, that could be never.

"I guess you're right," Fred said, a little subdued. "If I don't give her some decent flowers she won't go out with me."

"You know that's not the way Edith is," Charley said.

Of course, Charley knew Edith had no problem at all telling a man no, but it wasn't because she thought he was giving her inferior floral bouquets.

He suddenly worried about the roses he'd given to her. The florist had put those little caps on the end of the stems to keep them watered, but what if they didn't work right? What if those roses were already wilting? Or turning brown?

He'd taken a chance by getting her the long-stemmed red ones. They seemed the most romantic, but hadn't he heard somewhere that they didn't last as long as the yellow ones? Or was it the other way around? Or maybe it was the white ones that were puny. Charley finally understood why Fred was drawn to carnations. There wasn't much a man could do to ruin a bouquet of carnations.

"They have those carnations with the glitter on them," Fred said. "They're nice."

Charley guessed some men could find a way.

"I think they generally have those for St. Patrick's Day and things like that," Charley said. "You know, for centerpieces in banks and hospitals."

Charley hadn't intended to be helpful to Fred in his plans. But he couldn't let the man fail that miserably.

"I thought maybe I'd get her some chocolates, too," Fred said. "If they're not too expensive."

Charley grunted. He'd thought of chocolate himself, but he had spent too much time at the florists looking at the different roses. Chocolate probably would have been the way to go.

"Doris June said her mom likes mint patties," Fred said. "At least it's nothing imported."

Charley didn't think they needed to worry about seeing any imported chocolate in Miles City anyway, but he didn't say anything. Fred seemed content with his plans and was mercifully quiet for the next ten miles.

"Will they have assigned seats at this harvest dinner?" Fred asked abruptly.

"Never have before. People just sit where they want."

"Then how am I going to be sure Edith and I are, you know, sitting together? Even if we come in together, I know she'll be up and around, talking to this person and that person. I think it would be better if she was assigned to sit next to me."

Charley had to give him some credit—Fred knew Edith's ways. "She's not the kind of woman you can keep down so don't even try, Fred."

Fred didn't look too happy with that answer.

Charley dropped Fred off at the florist and went over to Conrad's shop to pick up the headlight. Conrad had the boxed light waiting on the counter for him.

"That's not a woman's motorcycle," Conrad said as he handed his uncle the box.

"Jasmine seems to like it."

Conrad shook his head. "She probably doesn't know any better. I'll talk to her about it when she starts working here."

"Not sure I would," Charley said. "She's awfully fond of that bike."

"She'll see why others would be better. It's just a matter of explaining it to her."

Everyone seemed to be clueless about the women

of Dry Creek today. Charley left his nephew to his illusions and went to pick up Fred and—what was that—yes, his packet of flower seeds.

"You were right," Fred started in first thing. "They didn't have Gerber daisies. And then I saw this packet of seeds. Edith will be able to grow her own Gerber daisies. And she'll get a whole bunch of them. Isn't that better?"

"Well, I don't know," Charley said slowly, trying to decide how much to help. "There's time to get something else if you want. Weren't there even any carnations?"

"If Gerber daisies are what she wants, then Gerber daisies are what she gets. Nothing's too good for my woman."

"Whoa." Charley couldn't let that pass. "She's not your woman. So far, she's not even your date."

"She played checkers with me yesterday and said I had a knack for the game," Fred said proudly. "I think that means something."

Charley started back to the pickup. "It means she felt bad for you because you were losing so much."

"I didn't lose all of the time."

Charley unlocked both doors and opened his. He and Fred climbed into the pickup at the same time.

"Maybe I shouldn't ask her to the harvest dinner," Fred said as they pulled in to the lot of the grocery store. "Maybe it would be better to have her over to my place for a candlelight dinner."

Charley drew the line at candlelight dinners. He wasn't too worried about Fred asking Edith to the harvest dinner. For one thing, he knew she'd turn the man down. She'd be too worried about her biscuits to consider having a date for that particular event. He doubted she'd agree to a candlelight dinner, either, but Charley didn't want to chance it.

"I think you have a better chance with the harvest dinner," Charley said as they went into the store. At least in the well-lit church basement and, with all of the people there, it wasn't even likely that a couple could have much of a private conversation.

Fred grabbed a bag of generic mint patties.

"They were on sale," Fred said as he flung the bag of candy into their cart.

"Well," Charley said for lack of anything else to say. He was beginning to see why Fred had spent his life as a single man. He figured he had no reason to worry.

The two men were back in Dry Creek by noon.

Charley walked over to Jasmine's place and gave her the headlight. She promised to pay him back for the cost of it when she got her first paycheck. He said she should consider it a welcome gift to Dry Creek instead.

"I've never gotten a welcome gift before," she said, looking a little perplexed.

"You've never stayed in Dry Creek before."

Charley looked over at Edith's house as he left Jasmine's place. He could see that Doris June's car was parked out front and he didn't want to interrupt the mother and daughter. All he wanted anyway was to check up on the roses and see if they'd died overnight.

After Charley drove back to his house, he sat down in the living room. Yesterday, he'd unearthed all of the boxes he'd used in his last move and set them around the living room. He'd put off his plans to leave, but only until after the harvest dinner. He figured that whole experience would be enough to convince Fred that Edith wasn't the woman for him and he'd give up on his grand plan.

Once Edith was safe from Fred, he could leave, Charley decided. In fact, he should call Conrad now and ask if there was a place for him around the garage. He'd also need to rent a room somewhere. Maybe Conrad would let him bunk in his apartment for a while.

Edith wondered where Charley was. She'd walked over to his house twice this morning to ask him what kind of housewarming plant he would prefer. She'd already given him the jade plant as a token of friendship and she was leaning toward a red geranium as a housewarming gift. She'd decided that a kitchen plant was the essence of a housewarming gift and she'd always had her geranium plants above the kitchen sink.

Charley hadn't been home either time. Finally, she'd stopped at the hardware store and Les told her that Charley had gone into Miles City.

It was just as well, Edith supposed. Doris June had come by and they were getting things ready for baking all of those biscuits on Friday morning.

Edith had her ingredient list all ready for the trip to Miles City that she and Doris June would be making tomorrow. Her cookie sheets were laid out on the counter and she'd even checked her oven to be sure it kept a steady temperature.

She wondered if she needed a new timer and added that to her shopping list, just to be safe.

Each year for the harvest dinner, Edith made her baking powder biscuits, hoping the people of Dry Creek would eat them and remember the days when the town was just beginning. Biscuits were what people ate back then. First, the soldiers in the fort and then the cowboys who came—they all had their biscuits. Yeast bread was a luxury although she supposed there was some sourdough bread around. Mostly though it was jerky, hard tack and biscuits. Oh, and beans. That's what kept people alive.

She'd always been proud of the Hargrove name. One of her husband's ancestors, Jake Hargrove, had been an early settler in this area. Of course, he'd been a trapper so he probably had everything from rabbit to buffalo on his plate along with his biscuits. One thing was for sure—if he was a Hargrove man, he appreciated good cooking.

She wondered what Charley was bringing to the dinner. Last year, he'd baked several squash he'd grown on the farm. Since he wasn't on the farm this year, maybe he wouldn't bring anything. Not everyone needed to bring something. There was always an abundance of food.

Chapter Sixteen

"You can't just go up and hand the things to her," Charley said as he lifted his cup of coffee and took a sip. He was sitting at a table in the café with Fred. The early morning sun was filtering into the place and Linda was in the kitchen cooking their breakfast. "Women expect some sort of effort when you give them something. That's if you still want to bother with it all."

Fred had been asking Charley for two days now to give him advice on exactly how to ask Edith to the harvest dinner. Each time Fred asked, Charley refused. Until this morning. Charley had been sleepy this morning and he'd actually started to listen as Fred began his pitch.

And once he'd started listening, Charley realized that if he didn't give the man an ear, someone else would and who knew what they would say. So Charley sat there and tried to talk reason with the man. At least that's what he tried to convince himself he was doing.

"What'd you do the last time you asked a woman out?" Charley asked.

"I told her she had fine-looking teeth."

"Well, I guess that's a start," Charley said.

"She dumped me."

"Maybe you need to rethink all of this then," Charley said. "Maybe you should start with someone who wants to date. A woman like Edith Hargrove won't be easy. She hasn't gone out since her husband died, you know."

"What do you think she'll say if she won't go?" Fred asked anxiously.

"Well, I don't know what she'll say. And maybe she won't tell you no." *And maybe night won't follow day.* Regardless of her lipstick and new hairstyle, Charley knew Edith didn't intend to date any man. "Remember, it's not too late to spare yourself."

"I think the chocolates melted," Fred said. He had his hand clenched around the middle of the plastic grocery bag that held his flower seeds and chocolates. "I've got the seeds though."

Charley eyed the squished bag.

"Maybe I should try the chocolates first?" Fred asked. "See if they're still okay?"

"I don't think you should give her an opened bag," Charley said as Linda came out of the kitchen, bringing two of the breakfast platter specials to their table. "Better just forget the chocolates."

"I'll need to make another trip," Linda said as she set two big platters of food in front of them. There were scrambled eggs, ham, bacon and hash browns. "I'll be right back with the pancakes."

"Maybe you could answer a question for us first though," Charley said as Linda turned to leave. She turned back and he asked, "What would you think if a man gave you a bag of candy that had been opened?"

"What kind of candy?" Linda asked. She was suspicious already.

"Chocolate mint patties," Fred said.

"Did he do anything to them? Like those weird guys that inject poison into candy and stuff?"

"I wouldn't even know how to do that," Fred protested. "I just want to check them to see if they're melted. Or maybe stale."

"Why would you give anyone stale candy?"

Fred looked at Charley.

"Thanks for your input," Charley said to Linda.

Linda nodded. "Anyone want to try the new apricot syrup?"

"Sounds good," Charley said. He'd been hungry even before all of this heavy planning. He'd spent yesterday boxing up most of what he owned and by this morning he didn't even have a way to make himself coffee. He'd have to move to Miles City tomorrow like he'd planned or starve.

The problem was he still hadn't figured out how to tell people he was leaving. He didn't want to just stand in the middle of the street and announce it. He thought maybe he'd go by tomorrow and see Pastor Matthew. Maybe he could have a little notice put in the Sunday bulletin. After all, it wasn't like he was moving to the moon. He could come back from Miles City to visit anytime he wanted. He did not need to make it into a big thing even though he originally thought he did.

"Maybe I could cut the bag open just a little bit and then tape it back up," Fred said. "It would be bad if they were stale."

"Real bad," Charley agreed.

Fred nodded. "Maybe it'll help if I put a ribbon on it. Or some kind of a bow. A package should have a ribbon."

"Just be sure she's not carrying anything when you offer her your stuff," Charley advised. "She won't be able to take it in her hands and you'll just stand there looking like a fool."

On that one point, Charley was willing to actually help Fred. No man should have to feel that way.

"She's going to think I'm a fool anyway, isn't she?"

"Who knows what women think—especially that woman," Charley said. "I don't, that's for sure."

They were silent as they ate their breakfast.

"I need to ask her soon," Fred said after he'd finished his plate.

Charley nodded. "It's really too late already. The harvest dinner is tonight. You might be better off waiting for Christmas."

"Well, I tried to do it yesterday. She was never home."

Charley nodded. "She would have gone to Miles City yesterday to get everything she needed for her biscuits." It felt strange to Charley that he knew her schedule after all that had happened, like it should have been erased from his mind the minute she turned him down.

"I should have just given her five dollars and told her to buy her own chocolates," Fred said.

Charley grunted. The poor man didn't have a chance with Edith. Probably not with any other woman, either. "You do have a hobby, don't you, Fred? Something to pass the time?"

Fred looked at him blankly. "Well, there's checkers.

And I get the *Reader's Digest* every month and read it all the way through."

Charley nodded. Yup, Fred was in trouble.

Doris June had just walked into her mother's kitchen and set down the bag she was carrying on the table. "What a day. With all we have to do today, Brad decides he doesn't want to go to school. I had to practically drag him to the bus stop."

"I thought Brad liked school."

"It's not school. He's just upset because Conrad called Curt this morning and Brad overheard them talking about Charley wanting to work at Conrad's garage."

"I didn't know Charley was looking for a job."

Edith told herself she had been right that Charley had been lonely lately. She was surprised he hadn't mentioned his plans to her though, especially after she'd given him that card and all.

Doris June took five big cabbages out of the bag she'd brought. She and Curt had grown them in their summer garden and had set them aside especially for the harvest dinner coleslaw.

"I wonder if he couldn't work part-time at the hardware store if he wants something to do," Edith said. "That's make more sense than driving into Miles City every day. Although, if he does drive in, maybe Jasmine can ride with him."

Doris June set the last of the cabbages down on the counter. Then she turned and gave her mother a strange look. "Charley didn't mention any of this to you?"

Edith shook her head. "It's not like he doesn't already do some work though. Since Doc Norris moved to Florida, he gets calls on vet business here and there. That's work. Maybe he could just do more of that. The men all say he's very good, especially with horses."

Edith told herself she shouldn't feel slighted. Of course, she would have told Charley if she were taking a part-time job somewhere just because she would want him to know. But everyone was different.

"Charley's not just working in Miles City," Doris June said softly. "He's planning to move there. He asked if he could live with Conrad at first until he can find a place of his own. That's why Brad was upset."

"Oh." Edith didn't quite believe she'd heard right at first. But she looked at the sympathy on Doris June's face and she knew it was true. "Well, that's…"

Edith hadn't felt a twist in her stomach like that for a long time. There was the twist and then the pain that went right through her.

She had never thought Charley would treat her like she was unimportant, but he clearly was. He really should have told her. He was the first one she had told about Jasmine's letter. This was the awful part of love. Just because she thought of him first didn't mean he'd think of her.

"I can come back later," Doris June offered, "if you want to rest a bit before we start baking."

Edith shook her head. "We better get to work. I always like to have the food all ready in the morning so I can help decorate the tables at the church later."

Doris June nodded. "We're all a little upset, too. I know Miles City is close. But Brad likes to be able to get off the school bus in Dry Creek and wait at his grandfather's place until we pick him up."

"Maybe Charley shouldn't move then," Edith said. Her voice sounded hollow to her own ears. She couldn't expect him to stay for her, but he should certainly stay until his grandson was grown. "I mean, if he doesn't like the Jergenson place, maybe he could put in a trailer on that piece of land just outside of town. Or he could rent Elmer's house. Elmer just lives in the bunkhouse anyway."

"We can't tell Charley what to do," Doris June said.

Edith bit her lip. "Conrad sure is taking on a lot of help in that garage of his. There's Jasmine and now Charley."

Doris June shrugged. "I hear he's got nice used cars. Maybe business is good."

"Well…" Edith couldn't think of anything to say to finish her thought so instead, she took her large measuring cup and walked over to the new bag of flour they had bought in Miles City. She'd made jelly through her days of pain with Harold; it was only fitting she make biscuits after the news about Charley.

"How do I look?" Fred asked as he stood next to the counter in the hardware store. He was wearing Burt's suit jacket and Charley's tie.

"I hope they have good food there tonight," Burt said. "You're sure going to a lot of trouble to get to that harvest dinner."

Charley saw that his tie was twisting on Fred's neck just like it had done on his. It gave him some small satisfaction to see the man looking uncomfortable.

"I'm not going to wear this tie to the dinner tonight," Fred said impatiently as he ran his finger under his shirt collar. He had taped Charley's lavender bow onto his seed packet and taped the packet to the front of the unopened bag of mint patties. "This is just for me to go over and ask Edith to let me escort her. I'll wear jeans tonight."

"You don't even look like yourself," Burt said.

"And it's deceptive advertising," Les said. He was cleaning out a bin of bolts on a bottom shelf. "Shouldn't a woman be able to expect the same level of clothes when you go to the actual event as when you make your pitch?"

Les served as a volunteer sheriff in Dry Creek and Charley figured the man should have been a lawyer instead of a rancher.

"I don't think Fred needs to worry about being sued." Rejected, yes. Taken to court, no.

"Maybe I shouldn't give her the mint patties," Fred said with a worried frown on his face.

"If you ask me, you shouldn't even go over there. It's too late," Charley said.

Of course, Fred didn't listen. Instead, he turned to the other men in the hardware store. "Wish me luck."

"I'll pray for you," Les said.

Everyone, except Charley, gathered around the door to slap Fred on the back as he walked out of the store. Several of the men just kept standing there, watching Fred go down to Edith's house. If anyone expected to see him turn around, they didn't voice their lack of confidence.

"We're not going to be able to see him really ask her unless we walk down the street," Burt said.

"I don't think Fred would like us to spy on him,"

Charley said. He had no doubt the man was going to be humiliated.

Burt shrugged. "He'd do it to us, if we were the ones asking a woman out."

"I suppose," Charley said. Why did he feel like he was waiting to hear the screech of the iron wheels just before a train wreck?

Even though no one could see Fred after he turned up the sidewalk going to Edith's porch, they all still stood by the open door, staring down the street in the direction he'd gone.

They watched for a few minutes, until Les finally said, "It's crazy to have the door wide open and the fire burning away."

"This whole thing's crazy," Charley muttered.

Just then Fred reappeared. He was walking back to the hardware store.

"Well, I'll be," Burt said. Charley got up and crossed to the door. Fred lifted his hand in a victory sign.

Charley had to stamp down a quick rush of jealousy, but he managed to have a smile on his face when Fred stomped up the steps.

Until now, Charley had been planning to skip the harvest dinner and spend tonight packing up the last of his things. Suddenly he decided he should have one more good dinner before he left Dry Creek. And he still couldn't believe Fred was going to show up as Edith's date—he needed to see it for himself.

Chapter Seventeen

Edith had never been late to the harvest dinner before. Technically, she wasn't late for the actual dinner this time, either, she consoled herself. She was, however, late in delivering her food and helping with the final setup for the evening.

And it was all her fault.

She had been quite, well…surprised and hurt this afternoon when she'd seen the lavender bow on Fred's gift. It was clearly the same bow she'd taped to Charley's plant only two days before. She could even see the little piece of tape on the back of the bow right where she had put it.

While she had not expected Charley to press that lavender bow into some scrapbook and keep it forever, she did think that two days was an extremely short period of time to keep something that had any kind of meaning to a person. Some men kept laundry receipts longer than that. It didn't seem like it was asking too much that Charley keep a simple bow for a decent amount of time. A week seemed like the minimum to her. Two weeks would be even better.

She knew she shouldn't care about something so petty. But, somehow, the fact that she shouldn't care only made her more irritated until all of that irritation welled up inside her and she said yes to Fred's request before she even thought about what he was actually asking.

It didn't take long for reality to set in. She was standing at her open door, watching Fred saunter back down her sidewalk, when she realized what she had agreed to do. She couldn't call him back—not because she didn't try, but because she opened her mouth and nothing came out.

Finally, she closed the door and just leaned against it. What had she done? She had a date.

Of course, Doris June had come out of the kitchen to see what was taking her mother so long. When Edith told her, Doris June gave a whooping cry that would have startled her if she hadn't been in shock already from everything that had just happened.

"You realize what this means?" Doris June demanded.

Edith shook her head. She didn't want to know what it meant.

"We're going all out! Don't even think of taking Jasmine to the church with you. Curt and I will pick her up. And you're borrowing one of my new dresses—maybe the coral one that I was saving for Thanksgiving. I'm going to bring some of my makeup, too, and we'll do your face before you go. You're going on a date!"

Edith was afraid that's what it all had meant. The only good thing was that word of her date would quickly outpace the gossip about her marriage to Harold. People at the harvest dinner wouldn't want to talk about something that had happened forty years ago when they could talk about Edith Hargrove and Fred Wagner on a date right then and there.

That's why Edith had wanted to be a little early tonight. She wanted to get there before most people did so she and Fred wouldn't be making a grand entrance together. Of course, they were too late to be early or even on time.

Instead, there she was, a good ten minutes late, standing at the bottom of the stairs. A whole swirl of people were already there and half of them looked over to see who'd just come into the basement. When the church had remodeled the basement to make it into a fellowship room, people had worried there might not be enough light so they'd installed a generous number of fluorescents. A fly couldn't sneak in without being seen.

"Where do I put the biscuits?" Fred asked. He was directly behind her, dressed in his suit and carrying two big plastic containers.

They all had stopped talking when they'd turned to stare at the two of them so Fred's words were loud and clear. At first they'd looked puzzled—Doris June usually helped her with the biscuits. Of course, Edith knew what people were thinking now. Fred's suit alone announced that they were either on a date or going to a funeral later.

No man wore a suit to the harvest dinner unless he had been asked to get up and make a plea for money to fund some special project the church was planning.

It was always a big and unexciting project like reroofing the building. A suit always provided an extra nudge to people when they weren't eager to give to a cause, even if they felt they should.

Fred would have known about the suit-wearing traditions if he bothered to come to church more often. She knew he watched some television church programs, but that wasn't enough in her opinion. An able-bodied man who claimed to be any kind of a Christian should be in church on Sunday. Fred could learn something from Charley on that point.

Not that she wanted to start thinking about Charley now.

"The biscuits go on this table over here," Edith said as she started walking. The biscuits were always at the head of the buffet line, right next to the plates and silverware.

She hoped people got their fill of watching her and Fred as they walked down the aisle between the two main food tables, her in the coral dress with the fluttery sleeves and Fred in that dark, pressed suit. She noticed that the chatter started up again as they passed, but she couldn't decide if that was a good sign or a bad sign.

Fred set the containers of biscuits down on the table where she showed him. Edith hadn't trusted Fred with the breakable jars of jelly and she had carried them herself in a wicker picnic basket, which she set on a chair beside the table.

The table was almost full with the standard fare. The Elkton Ranch had provided big platters of roast beef, half of it done up with their famous barbeque sauce.

Mrs. Redfern had made her usual deviled eggs. Someone else had made scalloped potatoes.

"There are some little bowls for jelly in the kitchen," Edith said.

Fred followed her into the kitchen and half of the people in the room followed Fred.

"Mr. Wagner, how nice of you to come." Marla Wilkerson was the first to say something as she entered the kitchen, carrying a dish of spicy corn relish. "We always look forward to seeing you."

Edith opened a cupboard to look for the bowls she usually used for her jelly. She watched Fred out of the corner of her eye.

"Fred. Call me Fred. And I'm pleased to be here."

Fred was rubbing the inside of his collar like his tie had suddenly grown too tight. "I should get to church more, it's just that—that—"

"Don't worry about the past," Marla said sweetly. "We just hope to see more of you in the future."

"I expect you will," Fred said with a relieved smile. "Now that Edith and I are courting."

"Courting?" Edith gasped. She almost dropped the bowls she'd just taken off the cupboard shelf. Surely Fred was not courting her. Was he?

"Well, I guess people today call it dating," Fred said.

"Whatever they call it, I'm happy for both of you," Marla said, her face beaming until her cheeks matched the specks of red pepper in the corn relish she still held.

"But we can't be," Edith protested as she set the bowls in her hand down on the counter. "I mean we are *on* a date. That's true. But—"

It was too late. Edith knew that even before she saw everyone walk out of the kitchen. They were tactfully leaving her and Fred alone. Either that or they were on a mission to spread the word as quickly as possible. One way or the other, the difference between a date and dating was probably not a large one in their minds at the moment.

"How could you say we were dating?" Edith hissed once they were alone in the kitchen.

"Well, Charley said—"

"I don't want to hear what Charley said." Edith pressed her lips together. She could imagine all too well what that man had said. She wasn't even surprised that he was behind all of this nonsense. She wished she'd never given him that lavender bow to begin with. And he could get his own plant next time.

Edith picked up the bowls she needed and headed back to the biscuits.

Charley looked around his bedroom. There was nothing on top of his dresser and the closet was empty. He had one T-shirt that he hadn't packed away yet because he wanted to wear it tomorrow when he drove to Miles City. He decided it would be good enough for the harvest dinner. Christians weren't supposed to judge each other on their clothes anyway.

It was the shirt Conrad had given him last Christmas. It read For a Smooth Ride, Come to Nelson Motors. The lettering was white and the T-shirt black so Charley told himself that it was a step above the usual neon T-shirts he saw around. And it didn't advertise some rock star or bowling league. Nelson Motors was a good solid business and Charley was proud to let people know he would be working there.

When he stepped into the basement at church, Charley realized he had worried needlessly about anyone noticing his T-shirt. No one was even looking at him. The people sitting at the tables were all looking at Edith and his good buddy, Fred. Fred seemed to be having some problem with the metal folding chair he was supposed to be sitting in.

"It won't take but a minute to fix the thing," Fred said as he lifted the chair up. The tables were close together so he had to carry the chair over his head while walking sideways down a small aisle between two tables already crowded with sitting people.

"Excuse me," Fred said as he bumped someone who ducked quickly.

"Excuse me," he said as he nearly hit someone else with the leg of the chair.

Finally, Fred was at the end of the tables and he was walking as fast as he could in a straight line toward Charley.

"Come with me," Fred whispered as he passed Charley and headed for the door Charley had just walked through.

Charley obligingly followed Fred out into the small hallway at the bottom of the stairs. Fred was already sitting on one of the concrete steps, his head in his hands. The chair was leaning crookedly against the wall of the stairway.

Charley picked up the chair and looked at it. "Nothing wrong with this that I can see."

"You've got to help me," Fred said as he lifted his head.

"Well, unless there's some bolt out that I can't see," Charley said as he turned the chair around to look at it from the back.

"It's not the chair," Fred said. "I just used that as an excuse to get out of there. I'd already gone to the restroom twice and I thought people would think something was wrong with me if I used that excuse again."

"But why leave now? You haven't even eaten yet. Can't you smell that food? Even out here, my mouth is watering. I know they usually have this little program where people list the things they've achieved this past year, sort of the big harvest in more than crops—but—"

"I can't stand it," Fred said as he put his hand up and loosened the tie around his neck. "I don't think I can do this."

"I can't believe Edith is giving you a hard time."

"It's not her, she's okay. It's all the other women. They're being so nice to me." Fred looked up at Charley. "I feel like they're fattening me up for something. I never realized what a responsibility it would be to marry Edith."

"Marry!" Charley felt his heart start to pound. "You can't be thinking of marriage!"

"That's what I'm saying. I'd have to be in church every week and not just sitting in the pews. Someone asked if I was going to teach Sunday school with her. Do I look like the kind of guy who should be teaching

Sunday school? First graders, at that. I don't know anything about little kids."

"I'm sure no one would expect—" Charley cleared his throat. "Did Edith say anything about all of this?"

"She was filling up the jelly dishes," Fred said.

"Well, that's good." Surely Edith would have more sense than to think Fred would make a good husband.

"Maybe you could tell people I got sick," Fred said as he stood up and turned to walk up the steps. "I don't feel too good, you know."

"Don't worry about a thing," Charley said as Fred reached the top of the stairs. "I'll take care of everything."

Edith decided that the only thing worse than having a date at your side was suddenly not having a date at your side. People were looking at her like they expected her to burst into tears. Fred had been gone so long this time no one could possibly think he'd be back. She felt like getting up and announcing that she hadn't even wanted to have a date tonight, but she knew what that would sound like so she sat there and smiled as the Curtis twins finished a cute duet.

"I'm sure he'll be back," Linda whispered as she walked by Edith. There was a lull in the program and people were shifting around. "Maybe he just ate too much of that candy he was giving you."

"What's wrong with the candy?" Edith asked. The bag of chocolate mints was still sitting on her sideboard at home.

"Oh, nothing," Linda said as she stepped farther down the aisle. "He and Charley were just talking about some candy and I thought—"

Edith stopped smiling. If she ever got her hands on Charley Nelson, she was going to—

"Excuse me."

Edith didn't have to look up to know it was Charley.

"Is this seat taken?" Charley asked as he set a metal folding chair down where Fred had been sitting.

"Fred is there."

"He needed to leave," Charley said as he sat down. "This looked like the only place left to sit."

Edith looked out at the sea of faces. She couldn't see any other empty places around the tables.

"Well, then—" she said as graciously as she could.

"You look lovely tonight," Charley said. Even if Edith had tromped all over his heart two days ago, he still wasn't going to sit by and let her feel rejected by her date. "I'm sure Fred wishes he could have stayed. He didn't look good though and—"

Edith looked at Charley. "You don't have to pretend. Everyone knew he was leaving when he carried his chair out of here."

"Well—"

"I don't blame him." Edith waved any excuses away. "I'd have left myself if he hadn't beaten me to it. You'd think people here had never seen a couple on a date before."

Charley grinned. He suddenly felt better. "Gave you a hard time, did they?"

"Let's just say they were very eager to see if the two of us would hit it off," Edith said.

"And did you?"

Edith figured that was none of Charley Nelson's

business, but before she could say so the program continued.

"I want to welcome everyone here tonight," Pastor Matthew said. "As you all know, we're here to celebrate the harvest of the crops. Enough of us are farmers to know how important good crops are to our community."

There was a murmur of agreement around the room.

"Each year we have a brief time set aside for people to acknowledge any areas of growth that have happened this past year for which they are particularly grateful. We know our harvest is not only about our crops, it's also about our lives."

"I've got one," a voice called from the middle of the room.

Edith looked over to where Elmer Maynard stood. He looked as if he'd recovered from his cold. His chair was pushed back and he was standing tall. "I want to announce that I've had a lifelong dream fulfilled. I am grateful to have a daughter."

Amazed voices rang out from various places in the room.

"They're going to think his cold went into a fever that scrambled his brains and made him delusional," Charley muttered softly to Edith.

Edith didn't even answer; she just turned stricken eyes toward him. "He means Jasmine."

"But how—" Charley said. "He can't know."

Just then Elmer reached into his shirt pocket and drew out an old photograph. "My daughter's the spitting image of my sister, Irene."

Voices rose as people stood up to try and see the picture. Elmer started to pass it around.

Edith was the only one who noticed that one of those people standing up wasn't interested in the picture. Jasmine was heading out of the room.

"Excuse me," Edith said as she pushed back her chair.

"I'll go with you," Charley said.

Edith had to admit she always liked to have Charley around when there was trouble. She didn't slow down to tell him that though. She wondered briefly what she would do without him when he moved to Miles City. She just couldn't imagine her life without Charley.

Chapter Eighteen

Jasmine was sitting on one of the basement steps when Edith opened the door to the stairwell. Edith and Charley hurried into the small space and closed the door behind them. Jasmine was blinking hard, but she couldn't stop a tear from rolling down her cheek.

Charley pulled out a handkerchief and offered it to her.

"I never should have come here," Jasmine muttered as she took the handkerchief and wiped furiously at the tear. "Never ever ever."

"Well, of course you should have come," Edith said indignantly. "How else would we have gotten to know you?"

Jasmine looked up. "I'm not ready for Elmer to be my father. I was just getting used to Harold."

Edith stepped forward and then leaned sideways to put an arm around Jasmine's shoulders. "Well, a picture doesn't really prove anything. Lots of people look alike and they're not even related."

"If you want to be sure about your father, you'd need DNA anyway," Charley said.

Jasmine shook her head. "I don't think I want to know."

"Well, then," Edith said brightly. "There's nothing to worry about. You'll just be everybody's daughter."

"I can't be everybody's daughter."

"Why not?" Edith shrugged. "We certainly have enough spare parents and grandparents around here. We can all love you."

Jasmine thought for a moment.

"I still shouldn't have come," Jasmine said. "All I did was mess things up around here. You know, it's like on Star Trek when they go into the past and they're not supposed to change anything or it will mess things up. Maybe I wasn't supposed to come here and that's why things aren't going right."

"I don't know what you're talking about. You haven't messed up anything," Edith said.

"Yes, I have. Look at you." Jasmine leaned her head back so she could look up at Edith. "You are out on a date with that Fred guy when it's clear you should be with Charley here. You've gotten knocked off course, and it's all my fault."

"I don't think—" Edith said.

"You see that?" Charley asked, sounding better than he had all evening.

"Look, if I hadn't written that letter, you wouldn't have decided to cut your hair—you told me you worried about meeting my mother," Jasmine explained. "And then Fred wouldn't have decided to ask you out. And Charley wouldn't be moving to Miles City because his heart is broken and—"

"Whose heart is broken?" Edith asked. Things were

going too fast for her. "You must mean Brad's heart is broken. That's Charley's grandson. His heart is broken because Charley is moving away with no thought to anyone's feelings."

Edith gave a look to Charley just to show that she thought he should give more thought to his grandson. She noticed Charley was looking a little white.

"You know I'm going?" Charley asked, looking at Edith.

"Well, no thanks to you. If Doris June hadn't told me, I wouldn't have known until you were gone."

"I was going to tell you—I just knew how busy you were with the dinner. You had a lot on your mind with making all of those biscuits and your jelly. Besides, it's not like I'm never coming back," Charley said. "And I talked to Brad this afternoon. I explained that he could stay at my place in Miles City when there were basketball games at school. I think he's okay with me leaving now. He'll get to go to a whole lot more games that way."

"It wasn't Brad's heart anyway," Jasmine said. "Conrad told me the reason he was firing me before I even started was because he was hiring Charley—"

"Conrad can't fire you," Charley said. "I'm a volunteer anyway."

"—and he said Charley needed to get away from Dry Creek, because he'd been rejected by the woman he loved. I told him I understood."

"I can't believe Conrad said that," Edith said. "He was just making an excuse not to hire you. Charley doesn't have a woman he loves."

Jasmine turned her shoulder so Edith wouldn't see and mouthed to Charley, "Tell her."

Charley knew what Jasmine meant. But he just stood there at the bottom of the concrete stairs. The air was cold. The space was lit up with enough fluorescent light to turn a man's face green. One of the women in front of him was still leaking a few tears and the other was looking at him like he'd done something wrong. Jasmine was right though. It was his chance and he had to take it.

"There's you, Edith," Charley said softly, looking down at her. "You're the woman I love."

Edith needed to sit down so she lowered herself to the concrete step nearest to where she was leaning. As she sat, Jasmine stood.

"I'll see you later," Jasmine said, smiling slightly at Charley as she walked over to the door and quietly went back inside the main room.

"Are you okay?" Charley asked Edith.

"It's so sudden."

"Sudden! We've known each other fifty years."

Edith looked up at Charley. He'd been her protector and her champion. She knew he would fight lions on her behalf if she was in danger. But did he really love her? In that way?

"I proposed!" Charley said indignantly. He saw the doubts on Edith's face. "Right there in the middle of the street, in front of God and everyone. I asked you to marry me."

"It wasn't quite in front of everyone," Edith corrected him. "The street was empty. It's not like there were witnesses. Besides, I know why you did that."

"Oh, you do, do you?" Charley crossed his arms. "Why do you think I did that?"

"You felt sorry for me," Edith said. "The others in the hardware store were making fun of me a little, saying Harold might have had his reasons to have an affair, and you wanted to make your point that you thought I would be a good wife. The proposal was your way of making your point."

"Men don't propose to win an argument." Charley knew Edith was too proud to accept some proposal she felt was second-rate. He didn't blame her, but he didn't quite know how to convince her things weren't like they looked.

"Admit it," she said. "You wouldn't have proposed if the men hadn't said those things. You weren't even thinking of proposing earlier. I would have known."

"Oh, you would, would you?" Charley said as he held out his hand. There was one person who might help him convince Edith his proposal hadn't been because of what she'd overheard in the hardware store. "Come with me."

Charley led Edith into the basement room. He kept her hand safely tucked in his elbow. He wasn't about to let her go. Les Wilkerson had just finished listing an achievement and he was walking away from the microphone that was set up in front of the tables.

Pastor Matthew stood up and walked toward the microphone.

"Come," Charley said as he led a reluctant Edith forward.

"What are you—" Edith whispered as she followed him. "This better be about something you've achieved and I just need to witness."

"Don't leave," Charley said to the pastor as he and Edith neared the microphones. "This involves you."

The pastor gave Charley a curious look, but he stayed. When Charley turned and looked at his friends and neighbors seated around the tables, he saw curiosity on all of their faces, too.

"This better not be about my date," Edith whispered to him. "Everybody already knows Fred is gone. You don't need to advertise it."

"Pastor Matthew," Charley said. "Do you remember the day Edith got her hair cut?"

"Sure, it was last Monday."

"Do you remember the day she announced Jasmine might be her husband's daughter?"

"Of course, that was Sunday in church."

"Do you remember the day I went to your office and we talked about my friendship with Edith?"

The pastor looked nervous. "That would have been the Friday before."

"That's before the haircut and the announcement?" Charley wanted his case to be completely clear.

"Why, yes."

Charley continued. "Did I or did I not confide in you that I was tired of just being friends with Edith Hargrove?"

The pastor looked at Charley. Then he looked at Edith. Then he looked at how possessively Charley held Edith's hand. The pastor's eyes lit up and he started to smile. "Now that you mention it, that's what you did try to say all right."

Charley turned to Edith. "There's your proof. The pastor wouldn't lie. This is no impulsive offer I'm making and it's a completely selfish one."

Charley finally let go of Edith's hand, but it was only so he could kneel in front of her. Then he took her hand again.

"My dear, beloved Edith." Charley's voice was strong. "Will you marry me?"

"Oh, dear," Edith said. She'd never expected this. Never in a million years had she thought…of course, she'd hoped, but…never in a million years.

Edith reached out and touched Charley's face. His skin was worn and not as smooth as it once had been. His hair was graying. His eyes though, his eyes had never changed. They were steady. They were sure. He was her Charley.

"It would be my pleasure," Edith said quietly.

The whole basement was stunned. No baby fussed. No fork scraped a plate. Even the young boys in the corner stopped their chatter. Then the whole place erupted in cheers.

Charley stood back up. He looked down at his Edith. And he kissed her.

Edith felt Charley's arms go around her and she felt comforted and excited all at the same time. Her friend—her love—was going to marry her.

The whole town of Dry Creek celebrated that night. Someone even called Fred and he climbed out of bed to come back to the dinner to slap Charley on the back and wish him well. He told Edith that he hoped he'd played some role in this happy news. She didn't tell him that Charley had proposed even before Fred had decided to ask her out. Instead, she just said that she hoped Fred would find his own true love someday.

Fred scowled at that and went to the food table to get one of the legendary biscuits and some choke-cherry jelly. The plastic container was almost empty and the bowls which held the jelly only had a few tablespoons of the red sweetness left in them.

Charley was standing by the food table receiving a dozen congratulatory slaps on the back. At the same time, Edith was sitting on a nearby chair and a steady stream of her Sunday school children were lined up to kiss her on the cheek. They needed a little prompting from their mothers, but not much. They were unsure what it would mean for them if their teacher got married, but they decided the adults were so happy that it must be good news.

Doris June followed the children and she gave her mother a big hug. "I'm so happy for you."

Jasmine followed right behind. "Me, too."

Everyone was reluctant to leave that night. The joy of such good news made them each feel warm inside. Gradually, though, children needed to be put to bed and families started to leave. Then even the ranch hands from the Elkton place put on their hats and headed up the basement stairs.

Finally, Charley and Edith were ready to leave as well. Charley went to get the empty containers that had held the biscuits. Some thoughtful soul had put Edith's Mason jars inside the containers so he did not have to look around for them. He lifted the containers proudly. From now on, he would be the one to carry the biscuits to the harvest dinner.

Charley drove Edith home in his pickup. Then he

walked her to her front door and offered to take the biscuit containers to her kitchen.

Edith's heart finally calmed down when Charley entered her kitchen. The proposal at the harvest dinner had been the stuff of fairy tales. Her head was spinning with the romance of it. But here in her kitchen was where she and Charley had sat together on many evenings over many years. The kitchen was where their marriage would thrive.

"Would you like some tea?" Edith asked.

Charley nodded. "Very much."

Charley watched as his Edith put on her teakettle. She moved a little slower each year. He figured he did, too. Then she turned around to come back to the table and Charley felt the years fall away. He remembered the vulnerable wife she'd been to another man.

"I'll be a good husband to you," he pledged as she sat down at the table with him. "The very best I know how to be."

Charley reached out and took his beloved's hand.

"I know you will be," she said simply. "You've always been there for me."

"I know I might not be as exciting as Harold was," Charley continued. "He was a charmer."

Edith shook her head and Charley saw the love in her eyes. "I've never known a more caring man than you, Charley Nelson. Don't ever forget it."

Charley stood slightly and moved his chair closer to hers. Then he sat down and put his arm around her shoulders.

"And I'll be a good wife to you," Edith said as she felt Charley's hand on her face.

Charley didn't answer; he just leaned forward and kissed her.

The teakettle whistle started to blow, but neither one of them paid it any attention.

Epilogue

The wedding wasn't planned until after Christmas, but the suggestions started to flow in during October. Edith and Charley both agreed that the problem with being part of a community like Dry Creek was that everyone had an opinion about their wedding and felt an obligation to voice it, sometimes more than once.

People worried about what vehicle the couple would drive away from the church on their wedding day. Most of the men thought they should drive Edith's car, because it had become such a colorful part of the community over the years. Besides, they wanted to give Charley a hard time about having to take the woman and her car.

Their wives, on the other hand, pointed out that the old car had belonged to Edith's first husband—a husband who had betrayed her—and should be burned on a funeral pyre before the wedding. They made it known they would be happy to help with the burning. The only thing on which they all agreed, men and women, was that Charley's pickup wouldn't do in any circumstances.

People also worried about who should give Edith away at the altar. After some discussion among the men, Fred announced one morning, while sitting by the woodstove in the hardware store, that he was the proper one to give the bride away since he had given her to Charley that night at the harvest dinner and deserved some recognition for all the trouble he had endured to make this all happen. He reminded them he'd even worn a suit. And a tie.

Doris June, of course, claimed the right to give her mother away because she was, after all, the bride's daughter and only living blood relative. The difficulty with that, the other women pointed out, was that Doris June was also going to be the maid of honor and no one had ever heard of the maid of honor giving away the bride.

Jasmine, who was working at Conrad's place, offered to do the honors, claiming that it was only because she had interfered in the life of Dry Creek and written that fateful letter that the engaged couple were now planning the wedding.

Even the food for the reception was debated. The men thought the menu should include Edith's biscuits and jelly because they represented such an important tradition in the community. They repeated her own words about remembering the pioneers, but everyone knew the men only wanted more biscuits. They hadn't eaten their fill of them at the harvest dinner and they'd be without them for a whole year if they didn't somehow work them into the reception menu. Some

men, worried that Edith would be too busy after she
was married to make biscuits for the harvest dinners,
even volunteered to get up a petition.

The idea for the petition was quickly put down by
the women, though. They said no woman should have
to bake biscuits on her wedding day. Not even to honor
the pioneers. There was one suggestion that someone
else should make the biscuits, but everyone knew no
one made biscuits as good as Edith so that was as far
as the suggestion got.

Charley and Edith didn't venture too many opinions
themselves. They just met every evening and sat in
Edith's kitchen, drinking tea and making their own
plans for their wedding.

"We could elope, you know," Edith said one night
after she'd answered questions all day long about the
event.

"I've already got my bags packed," Charley said.
"We can go tomorrow."

"We can't go tomorrow," Edith sighed. "You have
the mail route."

Word had gotten out that Charley had been interested in another job and he had ended up saying yes
to a job as a temporary substitute postal carrier for the
rural route around Dry Creek. He was saving the
money he made for a honeymoon to Niagara Falls. He
didn't want to make the mistake this time around of not
taking his wife on trips and he'd found out that Edith
had always wanted to visit the falls.

"We could elope next week though," Charley said.
"I'm not on the schedule then."

They both just looked at each other. They knew

they couldn't get married anyplace but in Dry Creek, no matter how tempting.

"I draw the line at biscuits, though," Charley said. "I'm not going to have you slaving over a hot stove just to feed those men their biscuits."

Edith leaned over and gave Charley a quick kiss. "Don't worry about the wedding."

Charley grinned. "I'm not. As long as you say 'I do,' I figure the rest doesn't matter."

Edith would have told him he had nothing to worry about, but he'd leaned over to give her a kiss in return for the one she'd given him. There was nothing for either of them to worry about in a wedding day, she decided, not if it included kisses like these.

* * * * *

Dear Reader,

Mrs. Hargrove has been a supporting character in so many of my Dry Creek books that readers started to ask me to do her story. I hesitated because she is a little older than most romance heroines, but the Steeple Hill editors wanted to know her story, too, so I began to work on it.

As I wrote about Mrs. Hargrove, I learned more about her myself. I knew she was close to God, but, as I told her story, I realized she had to have gone through some desperate times to be that close. Her late husband's affair was the hurt that drove her into God's arms.

I know many of you who are Dry Creek readers have suffered equally hard times. I get handwritten notes telling me about some of the heartaches in your lives. Because of that, I hope the story of Mrs. Hargrove will give you, and all of my other readers, hope.

Renewed love doesn't have an age limit. It's not just for those people who are beautiful or drive elegant cars. Love can also come from some unexpected person.

I pray for you that you have the blessing of good friendship and love.

And, if you have a moment, send me a note. I always like to hear what you'd like to read about next in the Dry Creek series. You can write me a note and send it in care of the Steeple Hill editors at Steeple Hill Books, 233 Broadway, Suite 1001, New York, NY 10279. You may also e-mail me at my Web site: www.janettronstad.com.

Sincerely yours,

Janet Tronstad

QUESTIONS FOR DISCUSSION

1. Edith kept a secret. She told no one (except for her pastor) that her husband had an affair. Do you think she should have told her daughter, Doris June? If so, when should Edith have told her?

2. The Bible says children should respect their parents. Is it good to let your child respect a parent who doesn't deserve it?

3. Edith stayed with her husband after his affair. What would you have done? Did she apply any Biblical principles to her decision? If so, what were they?

4. Edith said that her marriage problems drew her closer to God. In your life, what things have brought you closer to God?

5. In a previous Dry Creek book, *A Match Made for Dry Creek,* Edith opposed her teenage daughter's marriage. Do you think her earlier experience in her own marriage prompted her objection?

6. Edith felt less of a woman because her husband had an affair. Have you ever let other people's actions make you feel less than you are? What did you do about it? What should Edith have done?

7. Edith finally told her old friend, Charley, that her husband had an affair. If a friend came to you and

told you that her husband was having (or had) and affair, what would you say?

8. When Jasmine Hunter, the daughter of the woman Harold Hargrove had the affair with, came to Dry Creek, she was hoping to find her father. Why do you think she wanted to know who her father was?

9. If you could have spoken with Jasmine, what Biblical principles would you have suggested she follow as she came into Dry Creek?

10. When Edith knew everyone was going to learn about her husband's affair, she finally told her daughter. Doris June didn't believe her mother. Has anyone ever told you something about someone you respected so much that you didn't believe what the person said? What did you do? What do you think Doris June should have done?

11. Edith was worried about what everyone in Dry Creek would think if they knew her husband had an affair. Have you ever done something that caused you to wonder if people would accept you?

12. Edith had been a widow for a long time when Charley fell in love with her. Why do you think it took her so long to see Charley's love? Has it ever taken you a long time to see something that is good news?

Love Inspired®

Playing Santa was not workaholic Dora Hoag's idea of a good Christmas. But how could she refuse Burke Burdett's request for help in fulfilling his mother's dying wish? Especially when all Dora wants for Christmas is a second chance with Burke.

Look for

Somebody's Santa

by

Annie Jones

Steeple
Hill®

LI87499

REQUEST YOUR FREE BOOKS!

2 FREE INSPIRATIONAL NOVELS
PLUS 2
FREE
MYSTERY GIFTS

YES! Please send me 2 FREE Love Inspired® novels and my 2 FREE mystery gifts (gifts are worth about $10). After receiving them, if I don't wish to receive any more books, I can return the shipping statement marked "cancel". If I don't cancel, I will receive 4 brand-new novels every month and be billed just $4.24 per book in the U.S. or $4.74 per book in Canada, plus 25¢ shipping and handling per book and applicable taxes, if any*. That's a savings of over 20% off the cover price! I understand that accepting the 2 free books and gifts places me under no obligation to buy anything. I can always return a shipment and cancel at any time. Even if I never buy another book, the two free books and gifts are mine to keep forever.

113 IDN ERXA 313 IDN ERWX

Name _____ (PLEASE PRINT) _____

Address _____ Apt. # _____

City _____ State/Prov. _____ Zip/Postal Code _____

Signature (if under 18, a parent or guardian must sign)

Order online at www.LoveInspiredBooks.com

Or mail to Steeple Hill Reader Service:

IN U.S.A.: P.O. Box 1867, Buffalo, NY 14240-1867
IN CANADA: P.O. Box 609, Fort Erie, Ontario L2A 5X3

Not valid to current subscribers of Love Inspired books.

Want to try two free books from another series?
Call 1-800-873-8635 or visit www.morefreebooks.com

* Terms and prices subject to change without notice. N.Y. residents add applicable sales tax. Canadian residents will be charged applicable provincial taxes and GST. Offer not valid in Quebec. This offer is limited to one order per household. All orders subject to approval. Credit or debit balances in a customer's account(s) may be offset by any other outstanding balance owed by or to the customer. Please allow 4 to 6 weeks for delivery. Offer available while quantities last.

Your Privacy: Steeple Hill Books is committed to protecting your privacy. Our Privacy Policy is available online at www.SteepleHill.com or upon request from the Reader Service. From time to time we make our lists of customers available to reputable third parties who may have a product or service of interest to you. If you would prefer we not share your name and address, please check here. ☐

LIREG08R

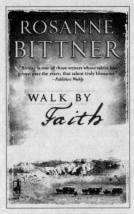

TITLES AVAILABLE NEXT MONTH

Don't miss these four stories in October

SOMEBODY'S SANTA by Annie Jones
His mother's dying wish has brought Burke Burdett back into
Dora Hoag's life. Together they have a chance to play secret Santa
for the less fortunate…and perhaps a second chance at the love
Dora thought she'd lost forever.

A MATTER OF THE HEART by Patricia Davids
Homecoming Heroes

Dr. Nora Blake's job is to save lives, not talk to handsome
reporters. But Robert Dale does seem to care for Nora and her
patients. Will his talent for getting the story be enough to win
him Nora's heart?

SNOWBOUND IN DRY CREEK by Janet Tronstad
Dry Creek

Rodeo champion Zach Lucas got more than he bargained for
when he agreed to play Santa and deliver gifts to widowed
mother Jenny Collins. Especially when he found himself snowed
in on Christmas Eve with a beautiful woman and a little girl who
needed help finding the true meaning of Christmas.

HIS LITTLE COWGIRL by Brenda Minton
Six years ago, Cody Jacobs left the woman he loved without
a second thought. Now a new Christian, he's come to make
amends—only to meet the daughter he never knew existed.
Cody struggles to become a part of the family he didn't know
he had. But Bailey Cross may not be willing to trust him with
their daughter's heart…or her own.

LICNM0908